Puppy Love:
2015

An Anthology Celebrating
Our Canine Friends

Edited By
Evelyn M. Zimmer

Puppy Love: 2015

An Anthology Celebrating Our Canine Friends

Edited By Evelyn M. Zimmer

ZIMBELL HOUSE
PUBLISHING, LLC
UNION LAKE MI

For permission requests, write to the publisher,
"Attention: Permissions Coordinator" at the address below.
Zimbell House Publishing, LLC
PO Box 1172
Union Lake, Michigan 48387
www.ZimbellHousePublishing.com

© 2015 Zimbell House Publishing, LLC

Published by Zimbell House Publishing, LLC
www.ZimbellHousePublishing.com
All Rights Reserved

Print ISBN: 978-1942818069
Electronic ISBN: 978-1942818076
Library of Congress Control Number: 2015934204

Photo Provided by Evelyn M. Zimmer

Acknowledgements

The production of this anthology could not be accomplished without the dedication and literary expertise of our Zimbell House team.

All Proceeds from the sale of this anthology go to Michigan No-Kill Shelters. Our deepest wish is that this anthology will help some of our furry friends to find permanent homes.

Our sincere thanks go out to everyone who submitted for this anthology, without you, there would be no new voices to tempt us.

Contents

Buddy's Birthday   9

Chet   15

Dog Days   27

Dog Days of Autumn   45

Dog is God Spelled Backwards   51

Doggie Pasha   67

Enter Wooly   81

Four Dogs, Fifty-One Years   93

Guardian Angel   101

Last Love   105

Lost and Found   113

My Angel Jake   127

Of Possums and Poetry   133

Olga, Mama and Mugsey   137

Pet Peeves   143

Philosophy of Dogs   153

Puppy Love   157

The Siberian Queen   183

Who Rescued Whom?   191

Contributing Authors   201

Buddy's Birthday

By Linda Carol Cobb

Where on earth was he? Buddy, our Westie, had vanished on his second birthday. His leash and harness were in the kitchen drawer, so Ed hadn't taken him on his daily walk.

We'd waited five weeks and five days, driven eight hours and paid $900 for a Westie puppy, and he barely tolerated me. It hurt my feelings. I was the dog person in this family, but Buddy was Ed's dog. He had Ed completely wrapped around his little paw.

The minute Ed finished breakfast, Buddy stalked him—even into the bathroom—and stared at him with big pathetic-looking eyes until he got his "W-A-L-K." If staring didn't work fast enough to suit Buddy, he started his string of sassy demands, "Ra, rah, rah, rah. Rah, rah, rah, rah, rah, rah, rah."

Buddy didn't walk. He crisscrossed from one mailbox to another—sniffed and peed, sniffed and peed, sniffed and peed. A skittish little dog, he was afraid to venture more than a block in either direction. If the

German Shepherds at the end of the road barked or the Collie with no voice box made strange raspy sounds at him, Buddy laid his ears back and raced home at Greyhound speed, dragging Ed behind. If we wanted him to walk faster, he'd put on his brakes and dig in. Ed compared it to pulling a shaggy concrete block with a leash.

I was glad Buddy and Ed had bonded. If they hadn't, this dog would have been long gone. Buddy chewed on our last nerves for a year and a half as he gleefully destroyed our plants, property and possessions. He played with dog toys for five minutes before anchoring them with his paws and shredding them into tiny pieces. A rugged toy marked "virtually indestructible" didn't last ten minutes.

At two, Buddy had finally outgrown his demolition stage, so we didn't have to check on him every five minutes. He still favored the forbidden furniture in the living room, over the old couch and chair in the den. He still pushed his bowl all over the kitchen in a growling frenzy when he was hungry. He still performed his head rubbing, body-pushing, strange-moaning dance every day. He wasn't a dog who would lay quietly in a corner. True to his White West Highland Terrier breed, he was smart and stubborn.

The problem was he was just too cute. Turning those brown eyes and black button nose up to us, he manipulated and trained us. Buddy ruled our house. With his pure-white coat of thick, wiry hair and perky, pointed ears, which seemed to have dozens of antenna positions, Buddy strutted his sturdy little body around on

Edited by Evelyn M. Zimmer

his stubby legs. When he wagged his thick tail, it thumped against the furniture and walls.

Westies were bred to be hunters. But not Buddy with his quirky personality. He'd spend hours barking at imagined threats, but he didn't like to venture outside alone, especially after dark. He'd fly back up onto the deck if a lightning bug lit up in front of his nose and scared him.

So where could Buddy be on his birthday morning? He'd disappeared. I searched the entire house again. I ran from window to window. I checked all his favorite hangouts. He wasn't piled up on the La-Z-Boy or the sofa in the den. He wasn't staring out the front storm door, his wide-screen neighborhood TV network. He wasn't toasting in front of the bar's heater, blocking the warmth from the room. He wasn't in his favorite illegal spot on the living-room recliner or in his bathroom crate or under our bed. I began to panic.

In the sunroom, I checked outside the sliding glass door again. I heard a noise in the garage. I opened the door and asked Ed, "Where's the dog?"

"He's in the backyard."

"By himself? That's a surprise."

Buddy wasn't an ordinary, play-in-the-yard dog. He had to be coaxed out—sometimes with treats. When he ambled out into the yard, he'd check to make sure one of us was standing on the deck. As soon as he finished his business, he'd dash back into the house to get another treat.

Our next-door neighbors were building an addition to the back of their house. Buddy would stand on the corner of the deck and bark at the workers. He didn't seem to like the loud machine noises, but the constant commotion aroused his curiosity. If no loud sounds came from the construction site, he'd venture over to the fence for a close-up view. Some of the crew would talk to him and pet him over the fence.

I hadn't heard any racket from the dog or the workers that morning, so I looked out the bedroom window. Four men were laying brick on the new section, but I didn't see Buddy.

Back in the sunroom, I scanned all the windows for any sign of the little critter. Nothing. Was the side gate closed? Sometimes Ed forgot and left it open, but it was shut. A movement caught my eye.

There he was. Whew...what a relief. I took a deep breath.

Buddy stood in the side yard with his nose to the ground. But what was he messing with? It looked like one of those ugly mushrooms that grew in our yard. Those menacing pinkish lumps popped up overnight. Some mushrooms were poisonous. None of our other dogs had ever paid attention to them.

Buddy sniffed the light orange object. He pushed it over with his nose. He picked it up. Oh, no! I pounded on the window. "Leave it!" His head jerked up as he heard me, and he dropped it.

Buddy lay down and started chewing on it. My heart stopped.

"Leave it!" I shouted through the glass.

Oh, my God! Our silly dog was eating a poisonous mushroom. He was going to die on his birthday. Without a robe or shoes, I tore out into the March chill in my green, nylon nightgown and white socks.

"Drop it! Drop it!" I yelled as I sprinted off the deck.

He grabbed the deadly mushroom and bounded around the yard full of pine cones and gumballs. I hopscotched in sock feet through the damp grass. My long, uncombed hair stuck out witch-like. The floor-length gown and no bra made it hard to run.

I had attracted an audience. The construction guys had stopped working. They were staring at me. No time to be embarrassed. I had to save our puppy. I chased our wayward dog. The closer I got, the faster he ran.

Dog obedience classes had been a waste of time and money with this terrier. "Buddy, sit! Buddy, stay!" I screamed.

Buddy reached the edge of the grass and paused before heading to the natural, over-grown back of the yard. He turned and looked at me. I stopped. "Drop it. Drop it!" I yelled as I stared him down. "Drop it!"

He opened his mouth and let the deadly mushroom fall to the ground.

Before he had second thoughts, I dashed over and snatched the thing up. Thank goodness. I'd saved our dog's life. I caught my breath.

I looked at the potential puppy killer in my hand. It felt different than the other mushrooms I'd plucked from our yard. I inspected it and realized why it felt strange. Oh, no, I've done it again.

Without glancing at my audience, I slunk back into the house. What were the workers thinking as they watched this scantily-clad woman chasing around the backyard and screaming at her dog? I'd put on quite a show with my unharnessed 38 DD's flopping up and down. How embarrassing.

Buddy followed me back into the house. In the kitchen, I opened the dog drawer and gave him a treat.

Those workers were the source of the problem. But they were just trying to be nice to a little dog. They didn't even know it was his birthday. Pulling out the garbage can, I dropped the half-eaten, glazed donut into the trash.

Chet

By Thomas Ford Conlan

Part One

In my usual pattern, I rolled out of the sack and stumbled toward the kitchen. A few beans spilled and scattered on the floor. The grinder whirled with the rich smell of coffee. I put the kettle on to boil over a low gas fire and groped my way to my study through the pre-dawn house.

Through the window, a whitetail doe stood nervously under a canopy of maple leaves at the edge of the ravine. I turned my head and she disappeared.

I lay on a woolen rug woven with images of ruffed grouse. Chet nudged his body next to mine. I reached my arms above my head to grasp the legs of the iron bench, cast with the image of another dog, not a Lab, and clenched the muscles in my arms.

Chet stared until I acknowledged him, his body still yet seemingly moving. I stroked the loose, thick coat hanging under his neck, kneading firmly. Chet nuzzled my ears and neck, taking care to keep his tongue away from my face, according to our longstanding agreement.

I stretched my back. He lay down beside me, also stretched, and we moaned in unison. I turned my neck toward him and breathed deeply. I love his natural smell early in the morning. Not the smell that comes after he snacks on fresh horse manure. On other days when he has been out roaming before stretches, I don't let him near.

I breathed and exhaled with my nose close, perhaps touching the sensitive hairs around his muzzle. He exhaled. We began an alternating rhythm for a few moments, maybe four or five breaths each. Then I laughed and told him, "Knock it off." He groaned. Best friends. No doubt.

The boiling water set off a whistle just as I finished loosening up. I poured the water through the ground beans, and fresh coffee plinked as it hit the bottom of the enameled tin pot. I let Chet out for a run. He refused to do his business in the cut yard, where anyone could see. He found the tall grass at the edge of the woods and looked embarrassed being watched.

My wife's sister, Becky came over early this morning to help with the barn chores. The girls like company and a chance for some horse talk while mucking out the stalls. Chet heard her truck turning off the highway half a mile away, barked, waited, and watched Becky drive up. Next to me, Becky is Chet's favorite person.

Becky's yellow lab "Belle" was Chet's dame." Sparky," Doc's lab, and a proven hunter, sired him. The planned union took a bit of doing. Sparky kept going for

 Edited by Evelyn M. Zimmer Puppy Love: 2015

the wrong end. Finally, the vet intervened. Chet was the pick of a litter of twelve. Becky and I put the pups through a series of sage, silly tests I found in a book about raising German Shepherds written by the Monks of New Skete. Chet won.

After Becky had finished feeding and watering the horses, Chet tried to climb into her truck. He knew, he smelled, her new lab was in heat. Or maybe he knew, he sensed, that Becky would be watching him with my vacation beginning the next day. Or maybe he just wanted to wander. Chet jogged alongside her truck down the long winding drive. Becky didn't see him, didn't notice as he veered off into the deep woods.

Chet refuses to recognize that he is growing older. He used to take off quite often. Not for any particular reason except his nose sniffing the air, searching for possibilities. I know that feeling. Distance created no obstacles in his friendly way, as he greeted everyone he met, especially, kids, attracted by their smell and their innocence. Still, often, I searched, worried. Sometimes I found him on his way back home. Sometimes a call came from the neighbor's place. Chet had been out visiting, trotting two miles or more, through the woods on a route like birds fly.

This particular morning I worried more. He could wear himself out if he wandered too far, especially in the deep February snow. I climbed into my truck and drove the back roads, slowly searching for his coffee beige coat. I stopped, hung my head out the window and studied the snow, looking for his tracks in places where his woodsy trails might have met the gravel road. I feared life without Chet though at times like these, he drove me to madness.

Last October, Doc and I walked along the grass field on the South Dakota prairie. Chet bound out ahead, too far ahead. He flushed a pheasant, out of range of a shot, then chased the bird single-mindedly while I yelled, urging him to stop. Doc hollered, "Tom, get that fucking dog under control."

I rushed ahead and got Chet's attention. He turned back to me, dejected and panting. I tied a line around his collar and silently, we walked the half mile back to the truck. Chet and I rested, sat in the long grass and shared a bottle of water while silently ignoring Doc's apology, three plumb roosters driven our way.

I turned the truck back home, and once arriving, waited anxiously, staring out the front window. A dark shape limped up the blacktop drive. I sighed in relief. My anger waned. Chet's step quickened as I walked out the front door. He probably forgot why he left and followed his nose to a new smell. Perhaps he wandered down into the ravine past the end of the drive, made it to the creek bottom, then on to the pond, spooking the mallards wintering there.

No matter, he was home, his execution stayed though I knew one day soon he would follow his wayfaring nose to a different end.

Edited by Evelyn M. Zimmer   Puppy Love: 2015

Chet

Dogs and Other Buddies

Part Two

I buried my buddy's bird dog today.

Doc had flight reservations to Jamaica with his newest version of a woman friend, a lawyer, and twenty-two years younger than the Doc." You should see her beautiful breasts" he says.

I do see her long curly blond hair. And the timeless sparkle of the Med in her blue eyes, her staring eyes, clear yet never focused.

The sky is dull and overcast this late April day. Snow is forecast, four to six inches. The world is tired of winter. We should all be flying to Jamaica. But then Doc calls with the news and asks, "My back is killing me and we're supposed to leave this morning, can you bury Zak?"

Zak was a hell of a dog. He ran as fast as lightning. Like most English Setters, he was goofy. He always had a neurotic expression on his dog face that translated into human-speak, "Pet me if you like, but I might bite you."

Doc and I hunted birds from the plains of the Dakotas to the thick woods of Northern Michigan. If Doc let him free of the line, Zak would shoot off like a rocket. In a scant few moments he was on the next ridge a half mile away chasing some bird or other, his silhouette dancing against the horizon. With a long cord attached to his collar but running free at the other end, Zak was art in motion. With his uncanny sense of smell, he stalked and pointed game birds of many colors, including pheasant, grouse, and woodcock. Back home on a walk in the park, his goofiness prevailed as he romped and pointed tweety-birds in the park.

Chet, my old yellow lab, and Zak's constant nemesis, jumped into the truck on my way to town. The two dogs fought so many times over the years, it was fitting that Chet be present in the end. Most of their altercations were caused when either Doc or I stuck a nose between the dogs and favored one over the other. Sometimes a fertile bitch would walk by and these genuine males naturally strutted to feign their dominance.

Over twelve years measuring eighty-four years each for Zak and Chet, Doc wore out three pickups to my two, as the four of us traveled.

October found us in South Dakota for pheasants. In Manitoba the last week of September, we chased clouds of ducks and fields of grouse. A weekend or any available autumn Wednesday meant a swing to the Upper Peninsula for a partridge in the heavy cover or just a long country ride. Zak, with his long flowing black and white coat, and Chet, stocky and golden brown, rode side by side in the comfort of the custom-made oak, dual kennel mounted in the pickup bed. They snarled, sensing the other's presence through the panel separating their dens. We fed and watered them one at a time. Otherwise, Chet would eat Zak's food while Zak postured and whined. A fight would usually ensue. After twelve years, Doc and I had the routine down pretty well.

I went along on the drive to the breeder in Harbor Springs when Doc first picked up Zak. Doc wanted me to drive home so he could lay on the floor with the pup. Doc slept with Zak in the outdoor kennel for the first week. His old bird dog, a setter named Jake had died after a long trip out west. The vet called the cause Parvo. I always thought it was the six shot in Jake's backside he earned for busting out some birds we had stalked for a mile. The shot didn't kill Jake right away, just slowed him down a bit.

I blew the afternoon off work to put Zak in the ground. I pulled off my blacktop drive, taking the pickup out in the fields for the first time that spring. Chet loped crookedly alongside the truck. I laid Zak under a choke cherry tree along an old gray fence line in an unused corner of my farm. The water table was high and Zak floated some in the hole until I covered him with moist, black dirt. Chet, having some trouble of his own in walking, sat in the long grass nearby and watched without expression while I covered Zak. A life is gone. Chet knows Zak is no longer with us. I covered the fresh dirt with a few field stones.

"No more bird dogs," Doc says." A time comes when you're too old to train another pup."

Time may tell a different story. Things may change when Doc returns home from Jamaica; when these cold April winds turn to the fresh days of September and October; when the world is an autumn field, with a buddy and a good dog at your side.

I buried my best friend's bird dog today. I still see the look in Doc's eyes when we lifted Zak into my pickup bed.

When a friend asks you to help him with his dog, don't ask questions.

Chet's Gone

Part Three

Chet died in the garage while I slept.

We both knew death was coming. These past few weeks he barked for no apparent reason. He barked at the silence, the only sound his old ears heard. He barked at the moon and the stars. He barked to keep demon death at bay.

The previous Saturday, I turned the garden soil. Each spring I renew the struggle to keep weeds away until the sweet corn comes. For twelve years, Chet watched and waited as I worked. He liked to lie on the grass by the edge of the garden until the sun grew too hot, and he found shade and cooler grass under the north eave of the house. But he always watched me work. He knew something good would be coming, but I don't think he knew when.

He ate vegetables. Tomatoes and cukes mostly. Some people say dogs are color blind. I doubt it. He knew when the tomatoes turned red. He knew when the cukes were fresh and green.

Chet was sneaky, always thought he was fooling me. He timed his raids strategically. He waited until I was out on the front porch or away from the farm. One windy day, winding my truck home up the long drive, I was greeted by corn stalks and silk spread across the lawn. He left half eaten cobs of sweet, raw corn, perfectly ripened; a cucumber mush with one bite taken, and mashed, partially eaten tomatoes strewn about, seeds everywhere. Volunteer plants and more weeds would soon follow. Chet knew how mad I was inside and would cower and hide with a helpless innocent look betraying his lying thoughts, "I'm just a dumb dog. I don't know any better." A few days later, I would return home to a similar scene and all I could do was smile and pick up corn silk.

Chet liked to wander, and I generally didn't worry too much. Except in the fall, when brain dead deer hunters were around. From a distance, he could be mistaken for a small doe. A bullet from a high-powered rifle can travel a mile. Then there are coyote hunters who poison deer carcasses. Chet loved a good carcass.

I knew his time was near. He hadn't wandered lately, staying too close by the door. He seemed lost, not knowing what to do. Doggie

Alzheimer's maybe? He barked even though he couldn't hear himself. The porch boards would shake with his thunder." Why the hell am I barking?" he must have thought, "because that is what I do. Maybe I can conjure a car up the drive, like the old days."

The last year or so he had trouble climbing steps. Chet and I came up with a solution. I called him over and he pointed his snout up the stairs. I would reach my arms around his tail end, barely touching his crank while avoiding it at the same time. He kind of liked it, turning with a sardonic smile. I lifted his back legs while he walked up the steps with his front. Our own four-legged wheelbarrow race.

Chet was a strong swimming dog. He used his tail as a rudder. When he was less than a year old, just a pup, Doc and I were up in Manitoba hunting ducks. Chet took to retrieving so well it was scary. I didn't really train him; he was born an innate, natural retriever. I knocked down a canvasback with four shot from my over/under. The duck wasn't hit too badly, floating out in the ten knot river current, when Chet jumped in. Ten months old and not nearly strong enough for these conditions, I thought. By the time he reached the thunder duck, they were eighty yards downstream. The duck dove under the surface. Chet followed, taking three breaths, three times up and down again. On the last rise, he had the canvasback in his mouth and began the swim back up the current. I watched anxiously as time dragged. Finally, there he was at the marshy shore by my blind, dropping the duck at my feet. Wet and wagging, Chet smiled. I never worried about him much after that, that is, until these past few weeks.

There was no one to stretch with this morning, no one to wander in and lie down next to me. No loose skin and fur to stroke. No earthy goodness to smell. No thick tail to whack me while he wagged like a helicopter.

Chet, the only dog that was ever really just mine, made me young again. He simply knew more than I could ever teach. He was simultaneously tame and wild. Truly, a water dog, a yellow lab more light brown, with coffee dark streaks in his coat.

I buried Chet down by the fence line under a shady tree next to Zak.

They say dogs are like their owners. I hope so.

Photo Provided by Thomas Conlan

Dog Days
By Andréa J. Onstad

"Harl, I've been thinking."

"Now that's an event worth recording. I can see the headline, 'Nine-Month Old Pup Thinks!'"

"Very funny, Harl. I'm laughing out loud. See? Ha-ha."

"No need to get your rump-hairs in a wad."

"I will if I want, Harl. I will if I want."

"Oh, Puck, I was just teasing."

"You always hurt my feelings."

"Aw. Want me to lick the wound? Let's see. Where would your feelings be? Here on this nob on top of your head?"

"That feels good."

"Must be the spot. Eugh. Musty. Long time no bath, huh?"

"I hate baths."

"Don't say that too loud, Ma'll mistake you for a cat. Okay, all better now?"

"I guess so."

"Well then, tell Old Harl what you were thinking."

"Okay. Here goes. I was thinking, if I sit quiet beside the path with my tail churning tiny tornadoes like this, a stick held gentle in my teeth like this, and a great big grin curling my lips up around it like this, when the lady comes, if I oh so tender place the offering between her slender soles without a drip of drool upon it, then sit back lightly on my haunches expectant but adoring, my eyes all doggie goo-goo like this, I'll bet she'll throw it for me."

"Bravo! Bravo! A very poetic dramatization, Puck. But you lost me."

"Weren't you listening?"

"Of course I was listening, Puck. I mean I don't get it."

"What didn't you get?"

"I didn't get what the lady will throw for you."

"The stick, Harl! The stick!"

"Oh. The stick. Right."

"Geez. Well?"

"Well what?"

"Well, what do you think of my thought?"

"I told you. It was a very poetic dramatization. But flawed."

"What's flawed about it?"

"No matter what you do the lady is not going to throw the stick for you."

"Why not, Harl?"

"Because I'm going to get to her first!"

"But she likes me best. I heard her say so."

"Maybe, but I'm Alpha Dog. And no one can resist Alpha Dog. Ah, I can feel her petting my silky fur, scratching my ears and you, lost waif begging by the wayside..."

"No! No! No!"

"Quit whining. Hurts my ears."

"But I can't stand it, Harl."

"Shut up, Puck. Anyway, you could never sit quietly beside the path. Never."

"Harl, I'm tired of your growl. You're all growl and no bite."

"Oh yeah? See these teeth? They could clamp down on your scrappy ruff and shake you to Doggie Doom."

"Get away from me, Harl. Your breath stinks. Hey Harl. Look at the Frisbee."

"Where? Where?"

"Over there, Harl. Over there."

"Oh Frisbees. I love Frisbees."

"Dumb mutt."

"What did you call me, Puck?"

"Nothing. Didn't call you nothing."

"Yes you did Puck. You called me a dumb mutt. I'm not a mutt. I'm a Border Collie."

"Collie! I thought you were an old fat goat! Hahaha."

"You little punk. I'm going to get my teeth into you and..."

"Don't get your 'rump-hairs' in a wad, Harl. Ha-ha. That was a good one. Back at you. Hahaha. Can't catch me. Ha-ha. Can't catch me."

"I'm not trying to, Puck."

"Because you can't, Harl. You're too old and too fat."

"You might as well quit your panting and prancing, Puck. And suck up that drool. Ma would swat you."

"No, she wouldn't. Ma likes me best, just like the lady. And when the lady comes down the path she IS going to throw the stick for me. Just watch."

"That lady is nothing but a bag of rags smells like old cat."

"So what if she does, Harl. So what. Anyway, I think she smells like Kitty Heaven."

"I know all about your flawed thinking. Come here a second."

"Aw Harl."

"Come here and smell this footprint."

"That's sounds like work. I'd rather play."

"Get over here right now, Puck. I'm going to teach you something."

"Borrrring."

"You want to stay ignorant the rest of your life? Learning like this doesn't come in obedience classes, which you DO need, by the way."

"Okay, Harl. I'm coming."

"That's a good dog. Now. See this footprint, Puck?"

"Yeah. So what.'

"This is where the lady stepped in her big rubber boots last Wednesday."

"Really, Harl? I'm going to kiss it. I'm going to kiss and kiss and kiss it."

"Yeah, well, it might take you a while by the size of it. Slender soles my paw!"

"She's dainty, Harl."

"Right."

"She is!"

"All right, all right. Let's not make an Animal Control case out of it. Just get your nose way down in it like this."

"Aw, Harl, it's two days old. I won't smell a thing."

"Just do it, Puck."

"Okay okay.'

"Right there in the heel where you can get a good whiff."

"Quit pushing, Harl."

"I'm not pushing, I'm herding."

"I'm the herder. Aw, Harl. It stinks! It's making me sick! I'm gonna puke."

"That's right. It seeped right through the rubber and got all over your 'dainty' little lady."

"It's horrible, Harl. What is it?"

"We're talking minimum fifteen years of fleabag feline."

"What?!"

"You heard me."

"Whoa, Harl. I didn't know cats got that old. Sure wouldn't if I were around. Get it, Harl? Get it?"

"Shut up, Puck. You wouldn't know what to do with one like this."

"Oh yes I would, Harl. I'd hunt down that old stink, knock her off her satin sheets, get my lips around that tough, stringy neck, then sink my teeth into soft buttery flesh."

"Soft buttery flesh, my torn ear! More like a mouthful of fleas is what you'd get."

"Oh, bug off, Harl."

"Yeah, and may your fleas never lose their flavor."

"I wouldn't mind ring-dating that neck, fleas or no fleas."

"Yeah? Well, you've got to watch the old ones, Puck. They may barely move, but they're real smart. And they've got claws as long as porcupine quills."

"Oh Harl, I want to go home with the lady and hunt cat! I do! I really do!"

"This one could kill you, Puck. I'm telling you."

"You ruin all my fantasies."

"I'm just trying to tell you, Puck. This fleabag's probably got the curtains and the furniture in the whole house all torn up and oooh baby I can just seeing her doing the cat trot all over the counters, drinking out of crystal goblets, eating off the plates, the silverware."

"The plates and silverware, Harl? I never heard of such a thing. Do they really...?"

"Yes indeed, Puck. This lady doesn't have any other pets. Or humans. Or anything. They get funny then. Especially the ladies."

"Why, Harl?"

"Smell here. Right next to that ant hill."

"Mmmmm, smells great. Like doggie-after-cat-lunch wipes."

"Get serious, Puck. All you smell is cat, lady, rubber and a little bit of lonesome. No dog. No goat. No kid. Not even another cat. Nothing."

"Aw, Harl. That means she needs me."

"Puck, this one will never have another pet. And she'll never never never have a dog. I know her kind. That lady hates dogs. She just pretends to like them. And she certainly is not going to let any smart ass pup—that's you, Puck—chase her little darling off the feather bed."

"Spoil sport."

"Grow up, Puck."

"Oh Harl, the great sage. I bow to your experience."

"Punk, see these long scratches across my nose?"

"You mean where you're turning gray?"

"Quit your sass or I'll nip you."

"Grizzle snout! Grizzle snout!"

"Shut up, Puck. You aren't so colorful yourself in all that black and dirty white. Now I'm trying to tell you something."

"Okay, okay."

"These scratches here come from a twenty-year-old puss. Half naked bag of bones, still as a statue, all matted up like a Rastafarian with bald spots."

"What's a Rastafarian, Harl? You use such big words."

"It's just someone with a real ugly hairdo, Puck. And boy was this one ugly. And did she stink! Whew! So there I was, young, green and tender, thinking she's too old to move, so I go up close to get a better whiff and she lets go with a two-pawed razor swipe combo so fast I didn't see it coming. It was a blur, Puck. A blur. That old 'pelagic had been just waiting to practice her right-left-right triple hook on some ignorant hound.

When she was done, she just sat there with her yellow eyes staring. Didn't blink once. It was chilling, Puck. Chilling. I was about your age."

"Yeah well, I really only want to play with the lady, not go home with her."

"Aw hell, Puck, I know you want to go home with her for a few days, chase pussy, get spoiled, and eat cat food. I've seen you looking over at her truck, that fancy new camper shell, that nice soft carpet in the bed. Nicer than Ma's truck. Even I'd like to get up in there and squirt a little bit."

"Bet that old cat would have a fit over a whiff of dog whizz in her palace!"

"She doesn't ride in the back of the truck, Puck. Get real."

"Still would be funny. That old wrinkled up sniffer and those whiskers wiggling, pure shock in her eyes."

"Ha-ha, Puck. Yep, it would. Ha-ha. Yes indeedy it sure would."

"Ha-ha yourself, Harl. I got the Frisbee. I got the Frisbee."

"See that squirrel over there on the ground, Puck? Right there by that tree? Ha-ha. Now it's mine. The Frisbee's mine. I'm Big-Dog-In-The-Yard. Look at me, Ma. Ma! Look!"

"Doggie fart. Doggie fart."

"Not me, Puck. Uh-uh. Not me."

"Yes it was you, Harl. See that big gray poof behind you?"

"Where? I don't see a big gray poof. Must've been squirrel tail."

"Ha-ha. I got the Frisbee now. Ha-ha."

"No, you don't. It's mine!"

"No. It's mine!"

"It's mine!"

"Mine!"

"Mine!"

"Ma!"

"Ma!"

"Okay okay. I'm bored now, Harl. You can keep the Frisbee. I'm going to get me a big pile of sticks for the lady when she comes. And she'll toss them for me and I'll run and chase and run and chase forever and ever. Oh, here's one. Just carry it gently, Puckie-boy..."

"Are you talking to yourself now, Puckie-boy?"

"What's it to you, Fat Dog. Yech! I hate it when sticks break in my mouth! Taste like rotten vet pills. Ish! Hate it! Hate it! Bleagh! Blaugh! Spit it out! Spit it out! Hey, how come you don't make stick piles, huh, Harl?"

"Two reasons, Puck. Two reasons. One, I hate the taste of sticks and two, I'm dignified. I don't go running after things. Not me. You're the one who goes running around in circles showing off, clowning, but no way am I doing that. No way."

"No Harl, you just go strut around the yard with that Frisbee in your mouth, think you're King Canine."

"You putting me down Puck? I don't like it when punks put me down."

"No way, Harl. I wouldn't do that. Not me. Look, Harl. Look at my big pile of sticks."

"That's not a big pile. That's a tiny one."

"Ha-ha. Fooled you. The Frisbee's mine now. Ha-ha. Got your goat and got your Frisbee."

"Here she comes Puck. Here she comes."

"Where, Harl, where?"

"Ha-ha. Fooled you that time. Ha-ha. Got the Frisbee."

"What's that? A little mange there on your back, Harl? Ha-ha. Got the Frisbee. Got the Frisbee."

"No, you don't. Not if I just. Take it."

"Ow, Harl. You're mblhurtblningmytbleeth."

"Can't tell what you're mumbling, Puck, with that Frisbee in your mouth."

"You're hurtingbljmytbltheeth!"

"Then let go!"

"No! Owblphg!"

"Give? Huh? Give?"

"Okay okay, Harl. I give."

"Punk pup. I hate it when you whine. La la. I'm Alpha Dog. Alpha Dog. Say it, Puck. I want to hear you say it."

"Quit it, Harl. I'm too depressed."

"Say it."

"Okay alpha dog. Are you happy?"

"I'm ecstatic, Puck. How about you?"

"You don't have to rub it in."

"Shape up, Puck."

"Oh Harl, she's never coming back."

"Hell, there'll be another just like her coming along any minute."

"Yeah, but no one smells as good of cat as her. Mostly city people come here. City people with allergies. They pet us and say we're cute then stick up their noses and forget about us. They hate us, Harl. Not her, though. Not her."

"Oh, Puck. You're so emotional."

"Oh, Harl. Her truck was gone when you and me and Ma got here. First time it was gone that early since she came here."

"Maybe she just went to town to get some pencils."

"Pencils?"

"You know, those yellow sticks she carries around."

"I could get her some yellow sticks. She didn't need to go to town."

"They're her tools, Puck."

"Tools?"

"You know, for writing. She's probably writing about us right now."

"I could help her do that, Harl. I know I could."

"Or maybe she went for an early swim. It's hot. Dog days, you know. Get it, Puck? Get it?"

"Oh, Harl. She wouldn't get into any nasty old water. Only Labs do that."

"Oh yeah? Yeah? I'm going to shove you right under the sprinkler for that remark, wash out that mold between your ears."

"Quit trying to distract me, Harl. It's not going to work. She's not coming back. Ever."

"Well, Puck, you know how they come in and out of this place, drawing and writing and taking pictures. There'll be another just like her, just watch."

"But Harl, she was special."

"She was special just because she was your first, Puck."

"But she didn't even say goodbye."

"That's how they are here."

"I can't believe it, Harl. I just can't."

"It's true, Puck. Get used to it."

"No, Harl. I can't."

"It's time for you to grow up."

"Ma!"

"Don't go crying to Ma. She's busy cooking for these fancy people."

"Ma!"

"Come on, Puck. Quit your whining. Here. Take the Frisbee. I'll run circles with you. Look! I'm a clown!"

"Ma!"

"Come back here, Puck! I'll even chase sticks with you. Here's one. Yech! Blegh! I hate it when they melt in my mouth!"

"Ma!"

"Come back!"

"Ma! Ma!"

"Oh Puck."

"I need you, Ma!"

"No! Puck! Don't tear the screen door!"

"I need you right now, Ma!"

"You'll get whipped!"

"BAD DOG! BAD BAD DOG! WHERE'S MY STICK."

"Stick, Ma? Stick? I'll get a stick. Stick. Stick. Where are you stick?"

"Aw, Puck."

"GET BACK HERE, PUCK!"

"Here's a stick for you, Ma."

"I can't watch."

"Ow! Ma! Ow!"

"LOOK. LOOK WHAT YOU DID. BAD DOG!"

Edited by Evelyn M. Zimmer

"Ow! Ow! Ow! Ow! Ma!"

"Border Collies. Nothing you can do."

Dog Days of Autumn

By Sharon Frame Gay

This is the time of year when all things seem possible. Mornings are misty, filled with promise, brimming with delightful scents on the breeze. I catch the trace of a female fox, cutting across our creek on the way to her den, a musty smell mixed with mother's milk, quick little prints across the muddy bank, then up into the woods, disappearing like a ghost trail. Scents stay longer on the lower notes near the ground, held in place by dew. I feel frisky, almost like a puppy again. Almost, except that there is something missing. There are times when I still gaze down the road, looking for him.

My name is Razz. Short for Razzmatazz, a name my people gave me, when I still had my milk teeth, torn from my mother's teat, carried home in a cardboard box. Those early days with my litter are cloudy in my mind. I belong here, now, to these people, the boy and girl, the woman. My family. And I belong to him, strong and kind, smelling of male sweat, pressed shirts, mints and a bit of tobacco. I am a Golden Retriever. Proud to wave my tail like a flag, proud to serve, to protect. I remember him saying something just like that, when he left that day, duffle flung over his shoulder, tears in his eyes, the long blast from the waiting train down by the station, mournful, foreboding. The woman cried hard and held him for the longest time on our front porch. Then, when he stepped off onto the sidewalk, she threw her arms around me and cried some more. I was already an older dog, then, but I stood as tall as I could, supporting her weight, head up, stoic, standing for her as long as she needed me. I was there for the children, too. When he left he said "watch over all of them, Razz", and I did.

I don't know where he went, but a lot of the men around here went with him. I kept hearing some words over and over again that sound like "Dubbya dubbya two" and strange names like Italy, Germany, France. Letters tumbled through the slot in our front door, smelling foreign, exotic, inviting. They crackled under my nose, and I was tempted to rip them up and eat them but I know the woman wanted them, waited for them, and somewhere, deep under the envelope, beneath the ink, I smelled him. I wagged my tail and looked out the window for him. I whined, scratched at the floor until the children called me away. "Come Razz, come play fetch" and we raced out the door and into the alley, tearing down the pathways after an old tennis ball that had seen better days.

The seasons went by, but I never forgot him. I missed him, wanted to play with him, feel his strong arms around me, around the woman, the little boy, and the girl. I have now taken it upon myself to raise the children.

Patient and kind, I sleep beside them on the bed, licking their faces and cuddling up so they stay warm during the cool nights. I growl at the postman, the delivery man, anybody who enters the yard and walks to our front door. It's my duty, and I take it seriously. I am the man of the house now, me, old Razz, and I am keeping it safe.

One day I growled at a young man on a bicycle as he pedaled up to our garden gate. He smelled of sadness and stress, office buildings and the oil of old typewriters. "Down boy," he said to me, reaching into his bag and pulling out a yellow piece of paper. "There's a good dog now" he murmured as he sidled past me. I sensed no danger on him and allowed him to pass, walk up the stairs, knock on the door, speak to the woman. "Telegram," he said gently, and the woman fell to her knees, keening, reaching for the door jamb.

My hackles went up as I stalked up the steps, bristling. What was this person doing to her? She was crying, reaching for me. "Oh Razz, he's gone missing! Missing in action"! I don't know what that meant, but I know that her heart was beating hard as she wrapped her arms around my neck.

The young man backed down from the steps, away from us, and I set to barking ferociously at him "get off my property", I howled in outrage. "Leave my people alone." Then I turned back towards her, and the children, as the whole world seemed to grow dim. Something happened. I didn't understand. Where was he? I need him here to help. I need him to hold us all. Then, I set my tail, held up my head, and got back to the business of raising this family. Just me. Just good old Razz.

Time went by, and with it the seasons. The children and I spent many lazy summer days in the creek out back, swimming and catching bullfrogs and crawdads. I sat on the bank in the sun to dry off, my fur smelling like wet wool, watching the kids as they ran back and forth along the rocks, buckets in hand, the woman not far away, sitting on a blanket, staring into the distance. Autumn came again, and I took the children to the school around the corner every day, my tail a plume as we stepped lively along the sidewalk, catching up with other children, all the little kids reaching down to grab my fur, patting me on the head. I stood like a good dog.

Then came Christmas, my favorite time of the year. There were dog treats and a new bed, too, and cookies that somehow found their way off the plate in the kitchen. I was stealthy. Took just one or two. Oh, but they were like happiness in my mouth! The best! And the tree in the living room smelled like the outdoors, like Frasier pine sap and birds. When I was a young pup, I lifted my leg on it, spraying my scent, just like I do outside. I got into trouble. The man dragged me out of the room by my collar and pushed me out the door. I was mortified. From then on, I treated that strange tree with respect.

Spring came, and with it baby bunnies for me to chase. I never tried to catch them. Just gave them a little thrill as I escorted them out of the yard. The earth smelled like birth, the sun on my coat felt like it had crept closer. But still, the woman sat, waiting, staring out the window, her hand on my head. "Good Razz," she would say "there's my old friend." I lay down on the floor beside her as she cried. My muzzle is turning white, my bones ache a bit, eyesight not as good as it once was, but one thing I can surely do is cry with her. I am getting old and starting to worry how long I will be able to be here, to take care of them. I whimper like a puppy.

And now it is autumn again. The air is sharper. Sounds travel farther through the leafless trees. Even the lonely sound of the train down at the station lingers on the air a bit longer, its whistle piercing the sky.

Something made me feel itchy deep in my soul when I heard that whistle. Not the kind of itch that a flea gives off, but the feeling of unrest when I catch something on the breeze. A scent. Like smoke and mints, only from far, far away, and something else, too. Something else that excited me raised the hackles on my back. I barked to be let out. I raced across the porch and down the stairs, turned in circles, nose up, sniffing the air, growling. Whining. Ears cocked, eyes everywhere.

And then...I saw him, walking down the sidewalk. Slower, much slower than he used to walk, limping a bit. The duffle flung over his shoulder, each step bringing him closer to me, to us, to the rest of our lives. The screen door slammed and the woman walked out behind me, peered up the sidewalk, a quick intake of breath, a stifled sob.

"Razz!" he cried. I let out a bark that shook the last leaves off the trees and ran into his arms. It is autumn, and all things are possible.

Dog is God Spelled Backwards

By Allan Rozinski

Amos's mother didn't tell him beforehand why she wanted him to go along with her to Willoughby family's farm. She walked there regularly by herself during the growing season to buy fresh fruit and vegetables, but Amos rarely went with her, as he tired easily and it became difficult for him to walk home. The strategy his mother had developed when she could talk him into going for walks with her was to have him take frequent breaks, sitting to rest until his energy reserve was built up again.

He'd been this way for as long as he could remember. The world seemed to be too bright and fast, everything loud and brash and in constant motion, with him left most of the time to look on helplessly. He could tell from an early age that he was a disappointment to his father, an active and impatient man who expected Amos and his mother to get up to speed or to step aside. His mother matched his father in energy, but when Amos looked into her eyes she did not avoid looking at him like his father did, but instead her eyes invited him to look. What he saw in her eyes was love tinged with a hint of sadness that she fought to keep at bay lest it overwhelm her in her commitment to him.

The Willoughby children, when they weren't being given numerous chores to complete, a fact of life for anyone who lived on a farm, were otherwise busy with some other occupation every time Amos had come to Willoughby farm. For example, Sarah Jane Willoughby was always inventing some kind of new variation on a game and getting most of the Willoughby clan involved, except for her two oldest brothers, who, on matters of principle, would not let their younger sisters or brothers determine the course of things on Willoughby farm. Already seeming to be fully-formed versions of what they would be as adults, they affected a more serious approach, becoming involved with learning more about the business end of farming, as they had experienced more than enough of the never-ending physical labor it required.

Since Amos was too delicate to participate in the robust physical activity that was normal for children his age, his friends were the imagined characters he read about in books. He was given a regular supply of reading materials by his mother, which she acquired in her travels by bus to the nearby town of Brandenberg, the closest town large enough to have a library. Amos's father always looked disapprovingly at the books that were stacked on the rickety bookcase next to his bed. His mother had salvaged the bookcase from a nearby home that had put it out on the sidewalk for nominal sale, which, had it gone unsold, would have likely consigned it to the trash heap; when she'd actually given the man who owned the bookcase some money for it, he grudgingly agreed to deliver it to their home. Rachel would peruse the books the library purged for sale, dickering and getting books for nearly nothing, as she and the library staff knew that most of the books would wind up being sold in bulk at the end to some secondhand store. She also was always on the lookout for books at sales of items put out after spring cleaning or when people put out items for sale when times got rough. The church Amos belonged to and his school also had occasional sales of books that he and his mother would routinely attend.

What a farmer would have done as a practical matter to an animal in Amos's condition would be to simply let it die if it could not be sold for a profit or offset its cost in upkeep through some job it performed on the farm. Lame horses that could not pull plows or even draw a buggy to town or to church would be sold to the butcher. Diseased or sickly farm animals would be shot, as they were a potential threat the rest of the livestock and had lost their value for sale. Or an animal might simply be left to fend for itself, such as the cats that people let go in the countryside that often wound up not being officially claimed by the farm families themselves, but did serve a useful function for farm families in that they eliminated vermin from damaging crops and spreading disease to the animals by stalking the mice and rats that sought the steady food supply the farms provided.

Dogs, too, had to earn their keep. They had to learn to alert the family when there were threats by people or animals who might come under cover of darkness to attempt to steal livestock or to plunder the harvest. They were rewarded with a status on the farm at a level just below that of the farmer's family and the farm hands if they were able to perform those valuable functions. However, Arthur McConnell was not a farmer. He and his family lived in the small home that had been part of the farm his family had owned at one time. The farm had been sold after Arthur's father's untimely death to pay off the debt still outstanding on the property. In an act of grudging kindness by the family who purchased the farm after the McConnells were forced to sell it, they had agreed to give the small outlying fringe of land and the small home second home on the farm to the McConnells to allow them to have a place to live and to grow enough produce to try to sustain themselves.

Arthur McConnell was a liaison between the suppliers of farm equipment and supplies and the farmers and suppliers themselves. McConnell's job was often a wearisome effort, as the farmers were, by nature, given to avoiding whenever and wherever possible the incurrence of debt while furthering the development of their self-sufficiency. Manure was rendered into fertilizer. Crops were rendered into feed for livestock. Seeds were cultivated whenever possible for the next generation of planting. The family members themselves worked the many and various jobs necessary to keep the farming operation going. But the loss of crops to infestation by pests or by blight required going to a second party, as it did when there weren't enough family members or farm hands available, or when farmers wanted to expand their operations. That was when equipment came into play.

McConnell worked long hours, although not has hard and long as the farmers did. His wife Rachel was a good woman, for the most part, except he believed that she should heed the Biblical edict that the woman submit to the husband. She had had a good heart, but for some reason his heart was colder and harder, perhaps because of what lessons he had learned from his father of the harsh practicalities of life.

Arthur McConnell did not know how to relate to Amos. He seemed to have walled himself off from the fact that Amos was his son. Whenever someone mentioned Amos's name or talked about him, or even if he had a thought concerning Amos, it was as though the core of who he was split off and watched the scene from outside, waiting for it to end so he could resume his life without needing to think about or acknowledge Amos's existence.

Rachel McConnell did the best that she could given the limitations of her circumstances. Her husband had a vehicle, a company bought truck that he used primarily for business and for some routine family activities on the weekends. Rachel depended on the county bus to get her to town; otherwise, she walked to destinations she needed or wanted to get to.

Rachel and Amos arrived at the produce stand the Willoughby's had out in front of their house. Sarah Jane Willoughby was sullenly seated behind the stand, having been assigned the task of selling the produce and canned and preserved goods, which kept her from her appointed rounds as the Goddess of the Variations of Games for other members of the Willoughby family and whoever else she could recruit among visitors to Willoughby farm.

"I hear that you have some puppies for sale," Rachel said to Sarah Jane. Amos stood at her side, spindly-limbed with braces on his legs, the shoes the braces were attached to looking like what Boris Karloff playing Frankenstein's monster wore in the movie Frankenstein.

"Why does he have to wear those?" said Sarah Jane, looking at Amos's legs.

"Amos is perfectly able to tell you that himself. Go on Amos."

"I had a virus that paralyzed my legs for a while after I was born," he said in a monotone, sounding as though he'd prepared a little speech to address such a question. "I was able to walk later with crutches, but I had some nerve damage. The braces support my legs and keep me from falling."

"Oh," Sarah Jane said off-handedly. She turned to face Rachel. "Queenie had a litter of pups. Mother put the sign up last weekend. All the pups are claimed and are going to go once they're old enough. Except for one."

"One left?" Rachel asked.

"Nobody wants it. It's got something wrong with one of its legs. Father said we should just drown it and put it out of its misery. Mother asked him to wait to see if anyone would take it first. He said it was just taking good milk out of Queenie's teat that one of the healthy pups could use." Sarah Jane shrugged and sighed and looked up at the blue sky, appearing hopelessly bored and seemingly invisibly tethered to the stand, the free spirit in her rebelling against such oppression.

"Let's have a look, shall we?" Rachel said to Amos. Amos followed her as she headed toward the farm house, walked across the front porch, and rapped her knuckles sharply against the screen door.

"Hello," Mrs. Willoughby called out from the hallway inside the house before arriving at the screen door and opening it. "Why, Rachel, what is it?"

"Hello Alice. We're here about the puppies. Sarah Jane said that you have one pup left. We'd like to see it."

"She tell you about the leg?"

"Yes."

"Poor thing. Joseph said that we should have gotten rid of it. What is it about men that they think that the way to fix things is to get rid of them? Makes me worried about what he'd do if I came down with a serious affliction." She hadn't noticed that Amos was standing behind Rachel. "Oh, I'm sorry. I didn't mean--"

"It's perfectly all right Alice. I know exactly what you mean, and so does Amos."

"Anyway, come on in." She opened the screen door wide, and they entered the rough-hewn farmhouse, sparsely furnished with pieces that were likely constructed by the Willoughbys themselves. In the second room on the right down the hallway from the foyer was a small room with a couple of ragged blankets lumped on the floor where atop them lay a female dog – a Boston Terrier – with swollen teats and a swarm of whimpering puppies suckling them, constantly moving their paws against her body almost like they were trying to swim. One pup was lay still and to the side of the other pups, all the other pups having access to Queenie. The pup that lay to the side of the other pups was small, its right hind leg looking stiffer and thinner than its other limbs. Mrs. Willoughby carefully watched Queenie to see her reaction as she reached for the runt, but Queenie was indifferent as Mrs. Willoughby slowly cradled the pup with her hands and picked it up to hold it.

"I put it near her when there is a gap now and then with the other pups, and it gets fed. Otherwise, I don't think it would have made it. It's still so small." The pup reacted with a yawn and a few small whimpers before going quiet again. "I don't know what will become of it. I'd just like to see it have a chance."

"May I?" Rachel asked, putting her hands out.

"I think it best that you don't," Mrs. Willoughby said. "Queenie's been willing to let me touch her pups, but when you have a crippled offspring, you never know what a mother might do in nature. I've seen them reject them, and if they do, it'll die for sure."

Rachel dropped her hands instantly. "I'm sorry. Well, Amos, what do you think?"

"What do I think about what?" Amos said.

"About us taking that puppy when it's old enough?"

"What about Dad?"

"Your father doesn't get to make all the decisions for the family. In fact, this will be your decision."

Amos could not help seeing the irony of the situation. If they'd come earlier in the week, one of the pups that wasn't crippled might have still been available. After all, what good was a crippled pup? It wouldn't be able to run and play like other dogs. It would certainly take more work, more looking after. He already had enough trouble getting through a day just caring for himself sometimes. And in spite of what his mother had said, he knew that if he brought a dog home without consulting his father about it first it wouldn't sit well with him, and that it would be just another thing his father would likely blame him for.

He looked at the pup. It was had a black-and-white flattened face a pink and black nose. It looked innocent, dependent. Amos somehow felt angry at and sorry for it at the same time, and he didn't know why. Why couldn't it have been born normal, without being lame so that no one wanted it? The problem is that if I don't take it, who will? He thought. And if no one takes it, Mr. Willoughby will kill it or let it die.

The last thought sealed his decision, for good or bad.

"Yes, Mama. Let's take him." Amos said.

"All right," Rachel said, then she looked at Mrs. Willoughby. "I can pay you now for him." She began to open her purse.

"Absolutely not," Alice Willoughby said. "He's yours. You just needed to say so."

"Well then," Rachel said. "Well. We'll be back to pick him up when its time."

"Another two or three weeks should be enough," Alice Willoughby said. "Come with me out to the kitchen where I can mark it on the calendar. We'll set a date."

****

After the puppy had been weaned by his mother with the persistent assistance of Mrs. Willoughby, Rachel and Amos McConnell arrived back at the Willoughby's farm on the agreed-upon date to pick up the pup. Amos had thought about the pup often over the last two weeks, but whenever he tried to imagine the pup actually coming into their home, an image of his father glaring with disapproval at both Amos and the pup would intrude into his musings and he would lapse into a generalized state of nervousness.

After Amos's mother had placed the pup in a basket she'd brought along to carry him home in and handed the basket to Amos, Mrs. Willoughby smiled. "I know you will take care of him, Amos. We've seen some tragic things happen when other animals have given birth here. Gives you a view on life that those who haven't grown up on farms never see. Makes you a bit harder, maybe. But this one burrowed into my heart. It's heartening when you see something or someone in life beat the odds when things are stacked against it." She lingered holding the pup a little longer, and tears welled in her eyes.

"Alice, you know you can see him whenever you want," Rachel said.

Alice Willoughby wiped her eyes with the back of her wrist from a free hand while she held the pup lying contently next to her bosom. "Yes, well, we say those things, but it doesn't ever really happen that way in life, does it? We're so busy here on the farm. But I will try to come see him. So silly of me." She ever so gently handed the pup over to Rachel, who cradled the pup like a newborn baby.

"You'll need some milk for him. I can give you some."

Rachel shook her head. "It's all right. I've got some milk at home."

"He'll need healthy food to build him up -- meat and vegetables. And Aloysius Dunn is the animal doctor if you need him. He's who all the farmers use for their livestock. He's good."

"Thank you, Alice," Rachel said. "Amos?"

"Thank you, Mrs. Willoughby."

"You're welcome, Amos. Take good care of him."

****

Arthur McConnell was not pleased to find that a dog now lived in his house when he returned home from a tiring day of haggling with farmers who were tight with their money and suspicious of everything he said. He wished that he could imagine a different way of life for himself, but out here in post-Depression-era in rural central Pennsylvania, where families were thinly strewn over vast acres of land, his job was, in a sense, like herding wild and often contrary cattle. But after the poverty and humiliation his family had endured after their attempt at farming failed, he had worked hard to develop his position in the territory to secure a livelihood for himself and his family. For better or worse, this would have been his life. His commitment to his family tethered him. And, what was more, his crippled son made his burden even heavier.

He decided not to confront the boy; instead, he would speak to Rachel. The boy would never have made a decision to bring a dog into this house on his own.

Rachel seemed to sense what he was coming. But he'd be damned if he wasn't going to have his say.

"Rachel—"

"Arthur, that dog is Amos's. He's our boy, but I am the one who is raising him, and it is apparent I am the one who will raise him until he's an adult."

"Don't talk to me that way. I put a roof over his head—"

"You put your seed in my belly. He's your boy."

McConnell was taken aback. Rachel could be somewhat opinionated and even a bit stubborn at times, but she'd never talked to him like this.

"He's out here in the middle of nowhere. He's missed a lot of school already, and I do the best I can here at home to keep him open to life and learning. He is going to need to figure out something else to do to make a living, and out here, that pretty much means farming and trades and services that cater to farming. Children can be cruel, and those who aren't will probably be, at best, indifferent. And what else would you expect a lonely and friendless child to become but a miserable adult? Is that what you want, Arthur?"

Sometimes because the days were so long and he was tired by the time he got home, he forgot about Rachel -- about why he'd fallen in love with her and why he'd felt lucky to have her as his wife. And here it was, clear as a cloudless, sunny day, why he'd wanted this woman. She had thought it all through -- what Amos needed -- and she'd made the best of things. He realized that he'd been doing nothing but feeling sorry for himself when it was Amos and Rachel who needed his support and sympathy.

"I'm sorry, Honey," he said. "I don't know what I was thinking."

"Be his father, Arthur. With a dog, he can forget about himself once in a while. When things get hard, at least his dog will accept him as he is."

"Yes. Of course, you're right." He felt ashamed of himself. Rachel came over to him and kissed him on the lips.

"That's the man I married," she said.

****

Amos had avoided coming up with a name for the pup because he'd had a fear that somehow something bad would happen and the pup would no longer be available. Several scenarios had played in his mind, including the puppy being killed impulsively by Mr. Willoughby before he and his mother could come to pick it up, or his father standing at the door of the home when they arrived with the pup, his arms folded over his chest and a scowl on his face, barring them from entering the house.

But nothing had come to pass to prevent the nameless pup from entering the McConnell house as Rachel and Amos, with Amos carrying the basket containing the pup, walked through the front door and into the hearth and heart of love that is the difference between the warm blossoming of life and the dark freeze of death -- at any time, and at any age. As fate would have it, the pup had been unlucky to be born lame, but lucky to have been found by those who would, in fact, love it all the more for what life had deprived it of, and who would to try to make up for it as well they could.

And isn't it the same for people? For we have all been crippled in life in some way at some time— figuratively, if not literally—and there is beauty to be found for those who discover a way to forget their painful memories and fear and instead celebrate the other side of life where joy can be found, if only for a moment, a day, or, for the luckiest among us, maybe for the rest of our lives.

The pup seemed unaware of its leg as an impediment: it used its leg to walk without any sense of self-consciousness or shame. And although Amos and his mother worried at first, the puppy frolicked and bounded about like any other puppy would. In fact, it could be said that the nature of the pup was play, and that play was life itself. The puppy's lame leg was strengthened with its activity, and Amos, too, had gained more strength and stamina in playing with the pup and seemed to approach life with less fear and more confidence as a result of the dog's example. Amos and others could not help but to admire, if not love, the dog it for its spirit, in that the dog did not let the leg become as an obstacle in its zest to simply live life in its expression of delight when at play or its desire to be a member of the McConnell pack that had adopted it.

Amos had called the dog "pup" for far too long, and his mother and father wondered at his stubborn insistence that the dog does not receive a name until it felt undeniably right and true to him.

And then one day, the name came to him, it being so obvious it made him laugh, the name perfectly suited to it. For when it ran after ball or a stick he threw and returned it to him, or when he called it to come to eat or to come to bed where it slept with him, it seemed to break into a smile and it express its happiness by running and bounding in a way that looked like a joyful skip. And Amos, armed with the lessons of love he learned from his mother and from Skip, was able to forge the foundation to face life in all its offerings laden with potential and disappointment. Skip lived with the McConnell's all the days of his life and was happy.

And for a dog, unlike for people, it was more than enough of a life.

Doggie Pasha
By Gary Beck

I couldn't take the soulful, accusing looks from man's best friend, my best friend, Pard, much longer. Yet, although his stress was increasing, my life was surprisingly stable. I was comfortably established in my East Village apartment in one of the few ungentrified, thus affordable, buildings on East 9th street. I still had my job teaching drama at Gotham University's School of the Arts, despite the enmity of the department chairman, Ernest the emoter, who I irked endlessly with my irreverent attitude towards authority. In one of my greater acts of self-discipline, I still strenuously resisted looking at the alluring thighs of freshman girls, amply revealed in short skirts. I ignored the periodic pangs of desire and left them to the seductive wiles of the predatory junior class lesbians, who had skillfully mastered the mechanics of roommate switching. I also continued to perform as a silent clown, outdoors on Central Park West and 72nd Street, weather permitting. This gave me tremendous satisfaction and contributed substantially to my savings, which were intended to produce my first full-length play, 'Unravelings', off-off Broadway.

My dog Pard, however, was not quite as well adjusted to his existence. I took him for three major park walks daily and fed him top of the line doggie food, supplemented with a fair share of my meals. This should have partially consoled him for the one glaring lack in his existence, the absence of intimate female doggie companionship. But it didn't. Whenever I brought a girl to the apartment, he stared at me reproachfully, already foreseeing that we would be doing the wild thing, which really freaked him out. As a young dog, Pard attempted to use me as a mating object. He would mount my leg, clasp me with his front paws, thrust against me until his red doggie thing was unsheathed, then sulk when I pushed him away. He next turned his affections on my visiting girlfriends, who were unanimously unappreciative of his non-romantic attentions and promptly departed in a huff.

It took me a while to really understand how important his doggie needs were, but then all my efforts to procure sexual gratification for him resulted in abject failure. I was still a virtual pariah at Tompkins Square Park, our nearby exercise area of choice, for aiding and abetting Pard's lustful assault on a fluffy Pomeranian. His depredation had resulted in his ejaculating on her well-groomed coat, to the indignation of her outraged owner and the righteous defenders who sprang to her side. One wimp, trying to score points, actually tried to organize a lynch mob. We were banned from the park for a month for that first offense. Thereafter, we were always scrutinized with the utmost suspicion, which effectively prevented Pard from even coming close to mounting a desirable female doggie. I sympathized with him, knowing he could see and smell that exciting doggie flesh, but not touch.

I tried many other ways to find relief for my faithful friend, who had once saved me from muggers and was always protective, a valuable quality in a sometimes dangerous big city. But none of my efforts on his behalf succeeded. Kissinger would have been proud of my negotiations on his behalf for sex. I had offered several owners money. I had even attempted to distract a number of female dog owners so Pard would have a chance to have his way, to no avail. It was as if female dog owners had ESP to warn them of the approach of a horny dog. I had searched in vain for a doggie pimp, (I guess procurer would be more genteel), but reluctantly concluded they didn't exist. My cleverest idea had been creating a newsletter, the Doggie Tribune, with a cunning personals column written by me to attract a potential sex partner for Pard and it was another disaster. It was also neglected for consideration by the Pulitzer committee. We received only one reply, a twisted, repulsive request by a disgusting degenerate to do perverse things to my best friend. This persuaded me to renounce the use of the personals column. My idea for a cable TV talk show to air the issue of doggie sex and find a sympathetic collaborator had foundered on the reef of insufficient funds.

My ex-girlfriend, Anitra, was a flighty know-it-all painter, the ultimate artiste, who created incomprehensible conceptual art that was so obscure that only her immediate circle of artist friends purported to appreciate it. She worked for the renowned Sophisto, the master of plastic, whose art consisted of wrapping man's and nature's finer creations in stifling sheets of plastic, to world acclaim. Anitra still maintained a well-regulated friendship with me that had survived my sardonic wit, often aimed at her master of plastic, as well as my lugubrious attempts to penetrate her chilly exterior. Anitra had no sympathy for my natural appetites, let alone those of my déclassé mutt. Her frequent advice, never considered by me for a moment, was to have Pard neutered. I suspected she felt the same way about me. In the absence of my accepting her smug, cutting edge solution to the distasteful problem, she urged sublimation to a higher ideal. Now I knew it wouldn't work with me, but it showed how other-worldly she was if she expected a dog to sublimate primal doggie needs. Sometimes it was crystal clear why we didn't connect.

Once again, I had only my own resourcefulness to draw on. This didn't help Pard, however, because no matter how hard I tried, I couldn't get him to understand that I was working on the problem. I didn't dare indulge in past fantasies about finding a doggie whorehouse, where for a few biscuits Pard could have his ashes hauled since he sensed I was daydreaming and howled miserably. Then, when almost at my wit's end, I read a newspaper article about luxury doggie hotels and just like that there was a possible solution. I decided we would check into a non-fleabag hostelry and by hook or by crook I would arrange a rendezvous, a tryst, an encounter, an assignation, a sensual interlude that would bring the victim of deprivation at least temporary satisfaction. Who knows? I might even enter into a dalliance with an alluring female doggie owner while Pard occupied her pet. Or would it be vice versa?

I immediately began online pet hotel research and lo and behold there were lots of doggie palaces offering the most outrageous luxuries. I couldn't resist snickering at the pretentious website of 'The Ritz Canine', a posh five star doggie resort and spa that featured caviar and filet mignon dinners, pedicures, a jewelry shop, a personal trainer and bedtime stories, all for exorbitant extra charges, in addition to the daily rate of $295 for a pedigree suite. This was so far beyond my budget that I felt like a French peasant listening to tavern gossip about Louis XIV's revels at Versailles. I had my first laugh in days when I visualized scruffy Pard cavorting in a hot tub with a pair of matched pink poodles wearing thongs. His disapproving gaze brought me back to the screen.

Now that I had another opportunity to help Pard, I got down to the serious business of identifying the right hotel. The first requirement was that it be affordable, then there had to be a way for Pard to be alone with the guest of his choice. I looked at websites for half a dozen hotels that all showed heated in-ground swimming pools, individual and group playpens, daily maid service, Swedish massage, freshly baked dog biscuits, costume parties and hot oil treatments. They offered accommodations in rooms, suites, bungalows and villas, all fully staffed. I couldn't help thinking about the homeless in America, struggling daily for survival in a society with insufficient social services for humans while the pets of the elite wallowed in lavish comforts. I idly wondered if these hotels had blue collar doggie staffs and could I disguise Pard as an assistant waiter or janitor?

In a moment of weakness, I called Anitra to ask her opinion. She was deeply immersed in preparations for Sophisto's latest project, wrapping Mount Kilimanjaro in colored spiral strips of plastic. She was her usual chilly, distant self and responded cuttingly: "Only someone with anti-social tendencies would consider something that vulgar and extravagant." I visualized her exposed on the north face of Mount Kilimanjaro, covered only by a thin sheet of plastic to protect her from the salacious gaze of local tribesmen. Then her frigid farewell brought me back to reality. After I had finished mumbling all the things to the disconnected phone that I didn't dare say to her, the conclusion was inescapable. Once again, Pard and I were on our own.

I was confident enough to believe that once we were legitimately established in the hotel I could find a way to get Pard alone with a female. Men had been liaising with women in hotels for thousands of years. Wasn't that how Socrates met Xanthippe? Then the first shocker. The obstacle that might be impossible to overcome. I finally noticed that owners didn't stay at the hotel with their pets. They checked them in and came back for them when their stay was over. Even if I could get past the desk clerk for an inspection of the premises, probably not an unusual request, there would hardly be time to make a doggie connection. It wasn't reasonable to assume that I could identify and suborn an employee who could be bribed to assist Pard in just a few minutes. Sudden clouds were now obscuring the horizon of hope.

I was too stubborn to give up a good idea that easily and decided to at least outline a plan... I would select a nice hotel, go there, of course leave Pard in the car... The car. I would have to rent a car. I looked at my budget, looked at Pard, remembered the hero of Tompkins Square Park, looked at my budget again, felt his mournful, accusing eyes lasering my back and decided to splurge. How much could a car rental cost? Then the second shock of the day. The cheapest operational vehicle, devoid of frills, was $100 a day, plus mileage, plus all kinds of insurance, plus GPS, plus on-board computer interface... The pluses went on and on and amounted to more than twice the rental fee. Was Pard worth it? Definitely.

I invited Anitra to join me for a drive in the country, but she obviously suspected an ulterior motive and scornfully refused, not even offering the excuse of plastic preparation. So one balmy Thursday afternoon in mid-October, following my morning classes, Pard and I set out for a jaunt to the Velvet Paws Country Club, an exclusive resort for the pets of the elite in Southampton, Long Island. The stress started at the Econo-Car Rental, where after a thirty minute wait, despite my reservation, the indifferent clerk offered me a battered Honda that looked as if it was salvaged from the Highway of Death. The car was filthy, the engine kept sputtering and the tires were worn. Scrupulous control of my temper, plus a twenty dollar honorarium, got me a Ford sedan in decent condition.

We headed for the Midtown tunnel, came out in Queens, a dreary borough, and got on the Long Island Expressway going east. It was a warm, crystal clear early fall day and the leaves hadn't begun to turn yet. The trees were a deep, lush green that contrasted dramatically with the sterile metal and concrete construction that uprooted nature. Pard had never been in a car before and he prowled back and forth on the backseat, poking his head out the window, doggie eyes bulging, taking in the new sights and smells as we whizzed along. Traffic was light and two hours later we pulled up in front of the guarded gatehouse of the Velvet Paws Country Club. It only took a few moments to establish my bona fides, I told them I was here for my employer, a noted Broadway producer, to determine its suitability for his Borzois. The guard looked doubtful, but phoned the command center or whatever they called it. Permission arrived and we drove into the hallowed grounds. I wasn't the slightest bit daunted by the posh surroundings and Pard certainly wasn't. His eyes, ears, and muzzle were working overtime, trying to take in everything at once.

I had read that the estate had originally been built by a prohibition bootlegger who struck it rich, then became respectable and didn't end up murdered in his swimming pool like the slightly unsavory Gatsby. The design of the main house was a tasteless confection of pink marble and pink stucco that defied simple identification with an architectural period. It was an uneasy amalgam of Bauhaus, Art Deco and MGM studios that strained the eyes of man, possibly even beasts. We pulled up in front of the shimmering entrance that would have served Tiberius' villa and a doorman in a green and pink uniform, with more gold braid than a French admiral, opened the car door and asked disdainfully: "Will your companion be staying with us, sir?" Having grown up in a household with the most supercilious butler in the western hemisphere, I wasn't the least bit intimidated." No. He'll just test the pH factor in the water before we leave." I ignored his confusion, said: 'Stay, Pard,' hoped he might and went inside.

The lobby was enormous with pink marble walls and a pink marble floor, as well as a pink marble reception desk more suitable for Hadrian's baths. I wondered for a moment if this was some kind of political or sexist statement. The impeccably green and pink uniformed reception clerks, one male, one female, both as remote as future android servitors, greeted me in unison: "Good afternoon, sir. May we be of service?" I gave them the 'here for my boss' routine and was surprised that they didn't want to phone him and verify my authenticity. Then I concluded that terrorists hadn't yet struck at the weak point of Homeland Security, the luxury retreats of the valued pets of America. My research on the web had revealed that sixty-three percent of the households in America owned pets. Granted, many could have been turtles or gerbils, but that still meant an incredible number of dogs and cats, whose owners would spend 38.4 billion dollars on them in 2006, 2.7 billion of that for grooming and boarding. That was more than the national income of half the countries in the world.

The female android clerk accompanied me on the grand tour of the dining room, the kitchen where they baked their own doggie biscuits, the tiled, in-ground, heated swimming pool, the recreation area, the spa, the music room, the spiritual retreat, and last of all the model suite. Except for its smaller size, it was as lavish as any luxury hotel. There were heated tile floors, a hi-tech ventilation system, picture windows, custom made furnishings, an orthopedic mattress and Ms. Android desk clerk informed me that a staff member slept in the room with the guest. Naturally they had veterinarians on staff, as well as a pet psychiatrist. She accompanied me back to the reception desk, where she gave me a brochure with the schedule of activities, then both androids chorused: "Have a good day."

I glanced at the schedule as I went on the long march from the reception desk to the resplendent portals. It made a summer day at camp Mussolini seem casual.

> *5:45-6:30 AM – Potty Time*
>
> *7-10 AM – Check In/Check Out*
>
> *7 AM - Room Service Breakfast*
>
> *9 AM-3 PM – Playtime, Swim Sessions, Ballgames, Hiking, Grooming, and Pedicure*
> *3 PM - Yappy Hour and Naps*
>
> *4-7 PM - Check In/Check Out*
>
> *5–6:30 PM – Room Service Gourmet Dinner*
>
> *7 PM – Baths and Massages*
>
> *8 PM – Evening Potty Time*
>
> *9 PM – Biscuits, Bedtime Stories, Pre-Sleep Music and Lights Out*

I had to chuckle as I pictured Pard, sly, mischievous and cunning, always looking for trouble, gracefully submitting to being treated like a doggie pasha.

The doorman, sneering at me, opened the door with his white gloves and tried several expressions of condescension. But I was a veteran of scorn from Ernest the emoter, whose repertoire outclassed a mere doorman, however gaudily bedecked. I opened the car door and Pard made his break for freedom and the good life. He was past me in an instant and dashed to a plump collie, moseying along with a personal care attendant. He easily evaded the PCA's attempt to grab him, nipped the collie on the flank, which produced an astonished yelp, then raced around the building until he was out of sight.

The invasion of the barbarian hordes took the comfortable, ponderously moving locals by surprise and they were slow to react to the hostile incursion. The doorman sputtered with indignation and his face turned bright red with choler. He couldn't decide whether to reach for his invisible halberd or succumb to a stroke. The absence of a rapid response team was evident and several green and pink clad attendants finally appeared and set out in pursuit of the rampaging Visigoth. Pard managed to nip several other aristocratic pooches, who protested volubly to their attendants, then he plunged into the heated pool and cavorted like a demented otter. I was particularly impressed by his aquatic ability since he had never been swimming before.

The defending forces converged on the pool and two of their bravest risked the perils of the deep. Just as they seemed to apprehend him, Pard put on a burst of doggie paddle speed and slipped past them. He scampered by the rest of the posse, paused to shake off vigorously on the doorman, then ran to the car, stopping on the lushest patch of the scrupulously tended lawn to deposit a pile of doggie poop that was definitely not the byproduct of filet mignon. I concluded that flight was preferable to volunteering sanitation services and we drove off, leaving behind an infuriated doorman, whose impotent waving fist was our last sight of the Velvet Paws Country Club.

Apparently no one had notified the gatehouse of our assault and vandalism because the gatekeeper waved a polite farewell as he opened the portals of freedom. Pard had his head out the window looking back contentedly at the havoc he had wrought, as the pink palace of pet dreams faded in the distance. He grinned at me so waggishly that I didn't have the heart to rebuke him for his crude behavior. Truth be told, that pretentious joint needed to lighten up a bit. I certainly hadn't intended to bring chaos to the palace of the privileged, but even Eden would be ineffably dull without a serpent.

But the paw writing on the wall was clear. Even a rundown fleabag pet hotel wouldn't provide Pard an opportunity for seduction or forceful violation. So I was out the money for the car rental and still was no closer to alleviating Pard's sexual needs. At the moment, however, Pard looked very pleased with himself and showed no symptoms of lack of doggie nookie. The look on the doorman's face, as we drove off, was partial consolation for another failure. It was frustrating not having anyone to tell about the day's adventure, but I knew that if I related the incident to Anitra I could foretell what she would say: "Ill-mannered, ill-bred and ill-disciplined." So I indulged in a brief laugh and stored the incident in memory. Then I renewed my vow to help Pard, who wagged appreciatively as we headed back to Manhattan, no wiser, but at least entertained by the afternoon outing.

Edited by Evelyn M. Zimmer Puppy Love: 2015

Enter Wooly
By E. Suzin Odlen

It wasn't love at first sight for me and Wooly. My husband's friend, Keith Stanton, was going to Florida with his wife and kids to visit his parents, when at the last minute, their dog-sitter had a change of heart. They'd exhausted all options before Keith mentioned the problem to my husband, Ted. "We'll have to put Wooly in a kennel," he said, "unless you and Suzi could watch her for five days."

"I'll speak to her about it," Ted said. "She might go for it."

"They'd have to put her in a kennel? That's awful," I said. I wasn't a "dog-person" at this point – I'd never even heard the expression – but I knew the dog slightly from occasional visits to the Stanton's, and I couldn't bear the thought of this exuberant animal being stuck in a cage. And so, nurturer that I am, I agreed to take in their well-trained, ninety pound, six-year-old Golden Retriever during their vacation. "She's no watch-dog," Keith warned me. "She'll bring the burglar a flashlight."

Wooly arrived with a box of dog food, some meager instructions, a few toys and a lot of hair, which covered the house in no time flat. First, I taught her to jump on our bed. She was very reticent to do so because she wasn't allowed on the Stanton's furniture, but I fixed that: I wanted her to sleep with us, cocooning, the baby I never had.

Ted had children from his first marriage. They were an integral part of our lives, but I didn't know them as babies. Nevertheless, I was glad to have a ready-made family. I didn't want to bear children; it required a leap of faith I just couldn't make. I knew if I had a child, I'd knock myself out, trying to be the perfect mother, but I didn't know with certainty that I could do the job to my satisfaction, or with any peace of mind. And if I couldn't handle it - well, what then? The element of luck involved felt staggering; I'm no gambler.

It wasn't an accident that I met Ted when I was forty-four. I thought I was safe; I wouldn't have to put my decision to the test. I'd always known on some level, that if I were to fall in love with a man who loved me back, I might have been persuaded to start a family, against my better judgment. Ted had asked me initially if I wanted

to "knock one out," convinced there was a skosh of fertility left in my middle-aged body. Perhaps there was a "skosh," as he was fond of saying, but I was very careful.

Over the years, Ted would tease me, "You're such a chicken! Little Sara would be ten years old already!" Time passed quickly. "Suz," he'd say, "Little Sara would be fifteen!"

But even when you make the best decision, it never feels totally right, and my maternal longings were, for the most part, unfulfilled. Enter Wooly, who serendipitously arrived shortly after I retired, when I needed her most.

The first night she was quiet and wouldn't eat dinner. I didn't know if she was feeling shy, bewildered, or just not hungry. Later in the evening, after Ted and I got into bed to watch TV, Wooly joined us. I brought her food into the bedroom and sat on the floor, feeding her. She ate kernel after kernel from my palm until she completed her meal. Then she let out a belch, a big one; it raised my eyebrows. I didn't know dogs belched – had never given it a thought, having never had one, but it endeared me to her.

As advertised, when someone knocked on the door, she didn't bark. She'd put a toy in her mouth and wag her tail frantically, waiting for the door to open. It could have been Jack the Ripper, as long as he petted her and played tug of war. But this was good for me, too. I didn't want a pit bull for a child.

At one-thirty in the morning, she woke me up by jumping off the bed. I liked the patter of her paws on the hardwood floor, but where was she going? I wondered, and then I heard her slurp, slurp, slurp. What a loud drinker, I thought, but the sound soothed me, like a fountain or lapping waves. She returned to the bed and positioned herself at the foot of it. A few hours later she rolled off the end and landed on the floor with a thump. When she jumped back up, I knew she was fine, but still. I realized I knew very little about caring for a dog, or I wouldn't have let her sleep so close to the edge. I felt anxious, unsettled. I didn't want a mishap while the Stanton's were away. Four nights to go, I thought.

Wooly loved to walk, I discovered, and in particular, she loved walking me, pulling me to and fro as we navigated the neighborhood. She made many sudden stops. And she changed direction at the speed of light, twisting my ankles. What could smell so good to her? I wondered, trying my best to relate, conjuring up the scents I adored: honeysuckle, lilies of the valley...or a pot roast in the oven. Clearly, she smelled something very different but try as I might, I couldn't think like a dog and she couldn't think like me. Still, it was fun hanging out with her, and more importantly, I felt needed.

When Wooly went home, I was still finding dog hairs for weeks. They fluttered in the air like snowflakes, blew across the floor like tumbleweeds, hid in crevices I never knew I had. And I really missed her.

"Have you noticed they put fewer tissues in the boxes?" I asked Ted after a day spent crying.

"Don't cry, Suz," Ted said.

"When she's here, she depends on me, Ted. I like it."

"I depend on you," Ted said, but we both knew it was different. Then he reminded me, "Wooly can come back for visits."

One night I picked up the phone and it was Keith Stanton, calling for Ted, although in the process of pleasantries, he casually mentioned, "Why don't you take Wooly a couple of nights a week when Ted's working? She's good company."

With a knee-jerk response of the heart, I said, "I'll do it!" A part-time dog! I thought. What could be more perfect than a part-time dog? Then I asked, "What about Wooly? You think she'd be okay with it?"

"She's a great traveler," he said.

"What about your family?" I said. "Won't you miss her?"

"We'll miss her," he said," but my wife and I work different shifts, and between taking care of the kids and trying to get some sleep, Wooly is alone for long stretches. I think it would be good for all of us."

I don't like driving a car, and certainly not with a dog standing on the backseat, but if I were to take her from the Stanton's to my house, there was no getting around it. Wooly, on the other hand, loved being driven in the car, her head out the window, ears fanning in the wind. "Lay down," I said, but she paid no attention to me. I could have been carrying explosives, that's how nervous I was, turning a five-minute trip into ten, careful not to make a sudden stop. This is a lot of stress, I thought, but that night I was relieved when she ate all her food from the bowl and jumped on the bed beside me.

For Keith Stanton, my taking Wooly a few nights a week was the wonderful break he'd envisioned, no middle of the night duty-calls, fewer dog-sitter problems, and less vacuuming. Wooly went back and forth between our houses, seemingly happy at both. I was the one with the problem. In a few weeks' time, the idea of a part-time dog, as exciting as it had been, was wearing thin. I was falling in love, and like any new mother, I wanted my baby close at all times, convinced that no one could care for her better than me.

Two months went by and with each visit, I lengthened her stay. Five nights! Then nine! The Stanton's didn't mind. They had two small children to care for, with a third on the way. And Wooly had trouble with their steps: she could go up, but not down. So she slept in the living room all by herself while the rest of the family was tucked into bed. As for myself, I had part-time children and a part-time dog. Great, I thought, but the lack of permanence or at least the illusion of it, was actually beginning to bother me.

The Stanton's had suggested on a few occasions that I keep Wooly. But how could I take someone's dog? I wondered, not fully comprehending that I already had. Then one day when I was dropping her off and she followed me back to the car and tried to get in... I knew she was mine.

****

If a dog can be sexy, mine is. Wooly is big and blonde and struts around the neighborhood like Marilyn Monroe on a leash, pulling so hard to greet everyone on the bike path, I'm afraid for my shoulder socket.

When we return from our walk on a hot day, she flops on the floor and starts panting, her breathing so labored, it worries me sick. I fold a cloth like a triangle and dampen it, then place it gently on her forehead, the point between her eyes. She cranes her neck towards me to make it easier, so I know she likes it. Then I grab my phone and snap a picture of Wooly with her cold compress. OK; a lot of pictures.

When she cools off and calms down, Wooly wants to lay in the yard. I put her on the run and place a fresh bowl of water beside her and plant a kiss on her mouth. Then I go in the house and try to relax, but my need to peek out the window consumes me. How could I have ever put a child on a school bus? I wonder, watching her basking in the sun.

One day I discover that Ted peeks out the window, too, but he's watching me, not Wooly. He sees me tickle her belly, her feet splayed in the air, doing a jig. "I see you in the yard with Wooly," he says. "I watch what you do."

And then he says the nicest thing: "You'd have been such a great mother." He's told me this before, but it's only been since Wooly that I believe him, and it means the world to me.

People who know me well say, "thank God you never had kids," and while I agree with them, it stings. And as for people who don't know me at all, there's a stigma attached to being childless. Are you selfish? Irresponsible? The word 'damaged' comes to mind. At the very least, there is something about you that is slightly off.

When Wooly's in the yard, I dash to the window every two minutes to check on her. It takes up so much time, it's hard to get anything done, but I can't stop. What am I checking for? Well, she might have an itch and be whacking her ear. She performs this action with such vigor I'm afraid she'll knock herself out. Or, she might be licking her privates until they're raw. I bang on the window to make her stop, and if this doesn't work, I open the window and scream: "Stop licking your cooch!" She stops.

One day there is a red fox in the yard, approaching her. The barking is so intense that I skip the window altogether and fly outside like a wild banshee. I put the fear of God in that fox, let me tell you. But my worst case scenario is this: Someone could snatch her – a thief, a dogfighter. She'd go with anyone, wouldn't put up a fuss at all, lover girl that she is.

And so, I've learned to like rainy days when she can't lay in the yard. "Bunk games!" I tell her, gleefully. That's what the counselors at camp used to tell us when we couldn't play outdoors. Back then, it meant marathons of jacks, cards, checkers and Pick-Up- Sticks. It meant eating red licorice and reading romance magazines.

Today, bunk games mean getting in bed with a pint of Haagen Dazs, cluttering the covers with books, programming the TV and taking a little nap...waiting for Ted to come home...and smooching with Wooly. Now, that's a perfect day.

I nickname her Mommy so I can hear the word out loud, since she can't say the word to me. She also goes by Twinkle Toes, Stymie, Love Bundle and Little Angel. She responds to all of them.

One night our friend, Sam, comes for dinner. Sam and I have screwdrivers and roasted vegetables while I prepare the meal, waiting for Ted to get home from work. Whatever I'm eating, Wooly wants it too, always, but we have our rules. For instance, dogs aren't allowed chocolate, so when I'm eating it, I say, "No, Mommy; it's chocolate," and she lays right down. Her obedience tickles me. I actually trained her to do something! So when she begs for a Brussel sprout, I say, "Mommy, you can't have Brussel sprouts. I put on too much seasoning; it will make you sick."

"Just tell her it's chocolate," Sam says.

"I can't lie to the dog," I say. We laugh, but this is the sorry state of affairs.

I have a running dialog with Wooly all day long. "I'm going downstairs to do the laundry," I tell her. She raises one eyebrow then the other. "And you think she knows what you're talking about?" Ted says, shaking his head in disbelief. "I know she does," I tell him. "We have a thing."

This "thing" keeps me very close to home. I resent anything that takes me away from her. Is my style cramped? I'll say, and I resent that, too, but I can't help it. Ted and I talk about it. "We can't even take a vacation, Ted. I miss seeing new places with you. Remember those olives we ate in Naples?"

"I remember," Ted says. "But look at it like this, Suz; if we didn't have Wooly, we could go away for two weeks, but then you'd have fifty weeks at home...without Wooly. Wouldn't that be worse?" His logic cheers me up. What a dear man I married, I think.

When Ted and I go to dinner with friends, he warns them when the menu comes: "Pick your dessert now if you plan on eating it. You know the dog's been alone for an hour! Suz is nearing her limit." Without question, I'm not the ideal dining partner. I can no longer savor the wine, pause between courses, and no, I don't want my coffee topped, either. Worse yet, I eye the server for the check – let's say – prematurely. Am I embarrassed? Yes, but I can't stop. Whether I like it or not, my truth is this, I need to be near the dog.

Like a child, Wooly acts best in a routine, and I'm not prone to deviate from it. In the morning, I prepare her breakfast while I brew my coffee. She knows "coffee first," and lies down beside me while I open the newspaper and enjoy my first cup – make that – half a cup. Wooly wants to walk; stomps her feet like a two-year-old. I ignore the behavior and gulp down my coffee, curdling my stomach. Wooly ups the ante. She adds barking to the stomp, convincing me – I'm ready for our walk. This is how parents give in, I realize.

In the evening, when I sit on the loveseat, we play tug-of-war. Wooly realigns my vertebrae - click, click, click - better than my chiropractor. But if I lay on the loveseat, she thinks it's time for her massage. She plops down in front of me, wanting her ears done first. After a few minutes of this, she rotates her body so I can rub a new spot. By the time she's done a complete 360, I've massaged her hips, head, spine, shoulder blades and under her chin, her head held high in the air.

One night, as Ted watches this act from his TV chair, he gets on all fours and romps around the living room, wagging his rear end like a tail! "Is this what I have to do to get your attention?" he says. So I get on all fours, too, and we cavort around the living room, thrilling Wooly, who loves this new game of slipping under our bodies, then jumping in the air.

Then Ted says, "Let's go for ice cream," and we pile in the car and drive to the Custard Hut. While Ted gets our treats, Wooly works the parking lot, sidling up to every stranger. So many people! So much ice cream! I guess that's what she thinks. I hold her cone when we sit at the picnic table. She twirls her long tongue, lapping up the vanilla ice cream. I inch closer to Ted, nestle my head on his shoulder. What a wonderful family, I think.

Four Dogs, Fifty-One Years

By Lisa Reinhardt

It was 1964 the year my older brother invited Socrates into our home. Less formally known as "Soc," he and I were about the same age in people years. Although just a young pup, he seemed a very wise old soul like his namesake. He had Beagle ears and a Labrador nose and a little stub of a tail that forced him to wag his whole lower half along with it. My brother carried him home in the box he was found in next to our Grandparents' house. To find a puppy in a box, for my ten-year-old brother was epic. Soc was never just my brother's dog though. He categorically became another—and possibly the best behaved—member of our family. Soc and I grew up together.

When I had the Mumps, with the innate compassion of Marcus Welby, M.D. Soc never left my side. And like the best-trained psychoanalyst, Soc could sit upright and listen to your problems without saying anything in return. I'm not saying Socrates was another

Rin Tin Tin, but in fairness, he really never had the opportunity to save someone from an oncoming train, or maybe he did.

When Soc and I were both seven, my parents separated. It was the `70's and my mother became a single parent. She also became paralyzed by the relentless grip of depression. Her station in life was transformed from wife and mother to staunch guardian of my father's vacant easy chair. I quickly learned that the glow of her cigarette in a darkened living room along with the sound of ice clinking in her lowball meant, "keep away." Soc and I were shipwrecked on a deserted island with no hope of rescue from the empty shell that was once my mother.

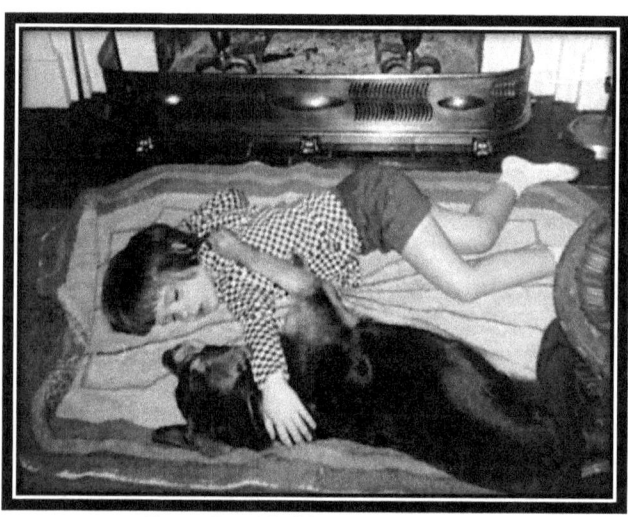
Photo Provided by Lisa Reinhardt

One year later depression claimed a victory and my mother took her own life. Soc became the keeper of all my secrets, confusion, and pain. We were together every minute. Soc was my source of unwavering loyalty and consistent affection during a time when the world around me was confounding and chaotic.

Over the years, Soc became a well-known character in our pre-leash-law little town. The butcher gave him leftover bones and the baker gave him day-olds. We knew this because when we went to pick up our groceries these proprietors would always ask us, "So how is Mr. Socrates doing today?" To which we would reply, "Well, he's fine thank you and if you see him, tell him to come home."

When Soc and I were ten, he made the front page of the local paper and there was community outrage after he was shot in the behind by our crazy, retired-cop neighbor. My father took the shooter to court and we won. After hours of surgery, our veterinarian told us there was nothing more he could do. Soc would never be able to urinate on his own and we should let him go. We decided instead to bring him home and three times a day my brother and I would carry him outside and help him relieve himself by gently pushing on his bladder. After weeks of this ritual, the day finally came when Soc was able to go on his own. This will forever be a most spectacular event in our family history, "The day Soc peed." Soc survived.

The night my very first boyfriend broke up with me Soc was waiting at the foot of the stairs when I got home. I sat and cried and told him all about it. Like a person who is learning a foreign language for the first time and can understand what's being said but is unable to reply in kind, Soc naturally had no words for me and yet I felt as though he understood every one of mine.

When we were eighteen Soc took a walk into the woods by himself and never returned. Our search for him was in vain. If we could have filed a missing persons report, we would have. I think what really happened was that he found a secluded place in the woods to take his final nap. It seemed so odd to me that he was just gone. No funeral or chance to say goodbye. I believe in all his wisdom he was somehow aware it would be easier on us for him to do this his way.

****

These days Molly is my roommate. She is a six-year-old black Labrador retriever and a career changed guide dog–which is the politically correct way to say she essentially flunked out of school. It is my opinion that Molly did not fail for lack of intelligence but because she is actually smarter than all of us. She found a way to live the good life and not have to work a day in it. She is my hero. She is here now, with her head resting on my foot, deep into a dream-filled sleep and snoring a steady low buzz that feeds me. I am comforted by her warm breath and by the knowledge that she needs to be so near. Molly and I have been family for five years now.

****

Before Molly, there was Lou. He was a black lab mix with soft cashmere ears and a big fluffy tail that was responsible for the demolition of many a wine glass. Like a feather duster on crack Lou's tail was in a perpetual wag. Lou was always happy and exceedingly low maintenance—the very best kind of roommate. With a dog as your roommate, there is no fighting over the remote control and the cap is always on the toothpaste. More importantly, it is impossible to fall out of love with a dog. Lou took very good care of me for thirteen years.

****

Before Lou, there was Sammy. She, like Molly, was a black Labrador, career changed guide dog who came to me by way of inheritance. Sammy was five when my father died of a heart attack. I considered her the very best part of my father's estate after his untimely death when I was twenty-four. In Sammy, I was able to keep a part of my father with me for another ten years. She moved across the country with me when I was thirty. She made me braver. When Sammy was fifteen, she had lost the use of her hind legs and it was time for me to say goodbye and let her go. I struggled with the reality that it was my job to end her suffering and thus enter my own. Losing her was like losing my father all over again. I felt gridlocked by a dark disorienting heaviness and that's when I realized that I had also inherited my Mother's depression.

I thought about times when I was little and would lay in bed at night and still feel the sway of the ocean even though we had long since left the beach. That's what it was like after Sammy was gone. I continued to see her in my peripheral vision only to turn my head and realize she wasn't really there anymore. I was shipwrecked again.

One month later I was introduced to Lou, a black lab mix in need of a home. At our first meeting, Lou plundered straight at me. He nuzzled my leg with his whole head then melted to the ground at my feet as if to say, "I pick you." There was no question in my mind Lou was now my new first mate. Lacking the wisdom of Socrates, Lou instead possessed the comic relief of Lucile Ball. He became my personal comedian with daily stand out performances that coaxed a laugh out of me again and again.

He was crazy for any kind of laser light or reflection. It was the game he could never win, the thing he could never catch. But with the persistence of a moth to a flame he never gave up. Lou was also a humper. Anything was humpable in Lou's world, my leg, anyone's leg, an ottoman; other dogs of course, though he had a knack for getting at the wrong end.

One day, I heard a short whimper coming from the bedroom where I discovered Lou in a most compromising predicament. While humping his own bed, he managed to get his penis stuck in the drawstring tie. The bed was essentially bound to his groin and the slightest move in any direction could be catastrophic. His eyes were huge with a mix of terror, embarrassment and stupidity. I was able to free him, but Lou just stood there, stiff and upright as though he had just been delivered by a taxidermist. Thinking on my toes I dashed to the freezer and grabbed a bag of frozen peas. After applying the bag to the area of injury, the look in his eyes instantly changed from panic to more of a "Thank all that is holy! Bless you! Bless you!" Exhausted by this calamity, he finally collapsed onto the carpet, where I left him alone to recover his dignity.

Lou lived to be fourteen and to the end he would routinely look up at me tilting his head from one side to the other as if to say, "Really? Tell me more."

Today, Molly is my comrade in arms, therapist, nurse and first mate. She is still a young adult so we have a good deal of time left together. It is indisputable however that my future will never be without a canine companion. I am addicted to the mutual and guaranteed unconditional love between a dog and its human. It is the truest of truths and with the deepest of gratitude that I can say in my fifty-two years thus far, my four dogs, Soc, Sammy, Lou and Molly have saved my life over and over.

Guardian Angel

By Gerri Leen

His name was Tiny. It was a joke because he was the biggest dog around. It wasn't clear who owned him; Tiny pretty much went wherever he wanted. This was back in the days before dogs only ran loose at dog parks, when dogs roamed free and nobody knew where they came from. Tiny strutted around like he was king of all he surveyed, his big black nose in the air, fur ranging from dusty gray to dark brown depending on whether he'd been lying in the dust or the mud. I liked him 'cause he'd walk me home from school and then the mean kids would leave me alone.

Every day after school, I'd hightail it into the little bit of woods that separated the elementary school from the junior high. Tiny would be playing there, making crazy games up with this collie-like dog I called Lad. Lad lived near the school, never ventured very far away from the woods, but Tiny would sidle up next to me, his paw pushing my hand up until I'd rest it on his head. We'd walk that way: Tiny taking brisk happy steps and me having to work to keep up.

But Tiny always slowed down when we got close to the mean kids waiting at the end of the walled cross through that hooked the schools up with the neighborhood. They'd be sitting on their bikes, looking real nasty, but I'd just keep on walking with Tiny by my side. Once the biggest kid pedaled toward me, saying, "Hey, boy, that ain't your dog."

Tiny growled. It was the deepest, darkest sound I'd ever heard. And he looked right at the kid as if he was sizing him up like the bike made no difference to him, or the fact that there were five other kids.

"Guess he is my dog," I said as I saw the kid back his bike away, his feet moving fast as Tiny just kept on growling.

And then Tiny and I turned like we were one being, and we just kept on walking. And after that, the mean kids didn't hassle me anymore.

When I was in fifth grade and the mean kids had moved on to high school, Tiny quit coming to meet me. I waited each day, sitting on the railing after school, but he never showed. My mom said maybe he got hit by a car. That he shouldn't have been running loose the way he did.

I checked the woods between the schools to see if he was hurt and hiding in the trees. Lad kept me company, but we didn't find Tiny. I walked all around the neighborhood streets ringing the school, trying to see if I could find a house where a big brown dog was tied up--

maybe his owners had gotten sick of him running around like he owned the world?

But I couldn't find him.

I wanted to call the pound. My mom got mad at me when she found out, said I shouldn't be bothering those folks when the dog wasn't even mine. But later I heard her on the phone, talking to someone about a big brown dog and had they seen it, and she sounded disappointed when they hadn't.

I looked for Tiny the whole rest of fifth grade and that summer after. I finally gave up when sixth grade rolled around. Even though I heard Lad barking in the woods between the schools, I quit going out to see him; it just wasn't the same without Tiny.

On the last day of sixth grade, they had a big ceremony for us, a send-off for junior high. Before I went home, I took one last walk around the school, looking into all the windows of the rooms I'd been in over the years. It wasn't like I'd never be back there--it was just the other side of the junior high, after all. But I'd never be here as a little kid again. I sat on the swings I hadn't been on since I was in fourth grade and thought about growing up.

In the distance, I could hear Lad barking. And then I heard a deeper sound. It sounded familiar and I started to run. I'd never run that fast before or felt my heart beat that hard.

I burst through the trees, into the little clearing at one end of the woods, and there was Tiny. He was scarred up, and he limped a little, but he still carried his nose high in the air like he owned the whole world. I dropped to my knees, and I was crying like a girl but I didn't care, and he was nosing me the way he liked to, flipping my hand up onto his head. I petted him with my other hand, and I could feel all his ribs. He had a cut on his ear, and his eyes looked funny. I stood up and said, "Come on, boy," and he followed me out of the woods.

I had to slow down to let him keep up. I'd have carried him, but he was still the biggest dog I'd ever seen. It took forever to get home, and Mom came out and took one look at Tiny and said, "I'll go to the store and get some dog food."

I never did find out who owned Tiny. No one ever came to claim him or put up signs on the telephone poles to say they'd lost a dog. He grew old as I grew up, and one day he lay down in the backyard and never got up again. I buried him by the fence, near Mom's rosebushes. She said a few words and I tried not to cry, but I did anyway. So did she.

I've had a lot of dogs since then. Dogs I loved, who loved me back.

I still miss Tiny.

Last Love

By Matthew Wilson

Jane was surprised when the postman rang the bell.

It was nice to get mail. Getting out the chair in stages, she shuffled toward the door, shivered from the early morning chill snaking in through the letter box.

"Morning," she smiled, fixed her glasses on her thumb-shaped nose. His hands were empty. There was no package, his manner hostile. Though she was a seventy-year-old widow, he'd come here for a fight.

"I want a word with you."

"Oh yes?"

"Your dumb dog took a chunk out me today. I want that thing destroyed. I've a job to do and I can have you fined for obstructing it."

Jane looked down, seeing blood stains on the postman's hairless shins. Shorts were no clothes for this weather, but even pirates had uniforms. She found it hard to get mad as she remembered him as a four-year-old, eating bugs in the mud, and time had not improved things. He'd never been happy.

"Maybe he didn't like your face. Were you fetching bills? You've yourself to blame, encouraging him like that."

"I want that animal out here, it's vicious."

"It's ninety-eight and blind in one eye," Jane said softly.

"Ninety-eight?"

"Dog years, dear. I doubt it's one tooth did that. He'd be more dangerous if you tripped over him, Darren. Are you sure it's my dog? There are many just like him around here."

"Don't call me Darren," he pointed to his official title on a stick back sided card plastered to his chest like a cops shield in low bold text she could not make out without glasses." Either you hand over that animal or I'll get my boss to take it away."

Jane gave the matter some thought and turned into the porch, "Harry? Did you do this awful thing?"

Darren saw two small eyes watch from the hallway, but there was no noise.

"There, dear, he said he didn't do it," Jane noted, if he wanted a cup of tea, then she'd be more than happy to indulge him. The wound looked quite sore.

"I didn't hear anything."

"Darren. Your mother would turn in her grave."

"I've had enough of this. I'm getting my boss and you'd best call a lawyer."

"Whatever, dear, but please come tonight, I'm more combative after my afternoon sleep. Shall we say after sunset?"

"I'll be here."

Jane waved once as he closed the garden gate behind him, limping till his complaints faded." Bye, Darren. Make sure you put some ice on that wound now."

As agreed, the three men came when moonlight fell over the small house.

"Gentlemen, welcome. Would you like a cup of tea—oh, here, Mark. Let me take your coat."

"Please, Ms. Hanson, we're on important business here. Don't call me, Mark."

"Oh. I remember when I used to babysit you and wipe your—"

"Right, shall we get on with it then?" The manager hung his hat up and made sure his papers were in order. "If there's evidence the animal is faulty, Ms. Hanson they'll have to destroy it."

"Oh, call me Jane, please. As I told Darren this morning, Harry wouldn't do that. He's always been a good boy and such nice company."

"Ms. Hans—Jane—please, we don't like doing this but when dogs were real people complained when their attacks forced us to stop deliveries on their street. There's a lot of scroungers round these parts and if they believed we couldn't post their food stamps—"

"You always were a silly boy, Mark. Stuffing crayons up your nose. Of course dogs are real, here, come into the living room. Look, Harry. We have a visitor."

The black Scottie terrier did not acknowledge the men as they entered the over-heated room. There seemed no life in him like an ex-partner purposely missing eye contact with an old flame.

Mark cleared his throat and told the mechanic to make certain. "Darren, is this—"

"That's him!" Darren stormed forward at a limp, fat gut sweeping one side to another and Jane feared he might knock her VHS collection from the wall. She was not comfortable with new -fangled machines. DVDs could go in the bin. She liked the old things.

"That's the little devil."

"Darren, please," Jane sniffed, and asked again who was for tea.

Mark found the right page on his notebook; he wanted this mess over with. As long as he'd known the old woman, the only thing she had to love was the dog. He didn't feel good taking it away. But if it harmed a human, it was toast.

"Boss, we got a problem here," the mechanic said and Mark followed.

"Huh?" Mark covered the distance in two long steps and squatted beside him, Harry did not breathe when the mechanic opened its mouth and found the wire.

Darren watched, demanding judgment, "You're not getting out of this, you old bird."

Mark looked at the mechanic, shrugged." Well, thank you, Ms. H—Jane. But we've taken up quite enough of your time. Come on, Darren. I think we've made fools of ourselves for one night."

Darren turned red as his fluorescent coat to warn early morning milkmen he was on the road. "What? But it was that rabid animal! It's a danger I say—you think I did this myself?"

Mark sighed, hating hypochondriacs. "I don't doubt a dog bit you, but not this machine. You see it's impossible. It's an old C-Z model, and they haven't made batteries for this in years. Any would have lost power before we were born. Jane—why haven't you upgraded Harry to sun power or plasma? He could be up and around in no time."

"Oh, no, dear. I couldn't do that, I don't trust these new things you know. And I'm not alone; Harry sits with me, keeping me company. He's such a good boy."

"Yes, of course."

"I still want paying for this," the mechanic moaned and throwing his bag of tools over his shoulder headed back to the van. Darren took more encouragement.

"I'll see you in my office tomorrow," Mark said, flushed with shame. Hopefully, Jane would not sue them for false allegations.

"But it was him! It was!"

"She'd have to throw that thing at you like a calculator to hurt anyone. It hasn't moved in years. Bye, Ms. Hanson."

"You sure I can't interest you in tea?"

"No ma'am. You'll get your post. I assure you. Good night."

"Good night."

Sadly, she closed the door and came back into her lonely home. Shame. It was good to have guests and talk to people from time to time.

Food she decided would cheer her up, so she settled on a plate of beans but before she put them in the microwave she opened a drawer and snapped open a small U.V bar, filling the room with strong purple light.

It didn't help her cataract, but the doctor claimed it a good way of getting extra sun on her crow's feet. She made a small oh sound as she saw the clock, realized her program started soon. The TV did not come on and she had to blow on the batteries in the palm of her hand to find some weak life in them.

The U.V light felt wonderful, filling her and many things with life.

"Wake up, sleepy head," she smiled, and Harry snapped awake. His raven wing colored tail wagged as his motors came alive like innards of an old clock. As programmed, he broke into a series of small yips.

"No, dear, this is people food," she sat down the steaming beans on one knee and patting her second, beckoned Harry on the other. Tail wagging he sprang up, settling in her lap, breathing at a quick, excited pace. He liked this show too.

"Tell me, dear and we'll never speak of it again...did you bite that poor boy?"

Harry looked at her with wide innocent eyes. As if to say, 'Me?'

She ruffled his head and pressed a button on the remote; the TV flickered and came on.

She liked the old ways, but sometimes for good things to continue, like Harry, arrangements had to be made. Converted. At first, she'd been uncertain when his old batteries had given out, but when the repair man brought him back from the shop in strong sunlight it was still the same Harry.

Still the only thing she loved, and could get love back from. She held him like a teddy bear, loneliness beaten back by his heated mechanical body breathing against her, with a sniffy nose.

"It's a good thing those young men came after dark, isn't it, dear?" She smiled and fell upon her food.

Lost and Found
By Priya Vennapusa

"If the boss catches you on Twitter, you'll be in big trouble." Carly placed her Starbucks cup on her co-worker's desk.

"Thanks Carly! Did you see this?" Tara was pointing to the image on the screen." You must admit that's cute."

Carly glanced at the picture of the handsome, dark-haired man holding a fluffy puppy and recognized Tara's favorite celebrity.

"Cute alright!" She looked Tara in the eye. "I mean the puppy. I don't understand why a grown man would want a little, fluffy dog?"

"It's a cockapoo and the tweet says he rescued it from the humane shelter. He's even bringing Justine on tour with him. Isn't that awesome? I can't believe he's actually performing here this weekend, at the Palace, and I don't have tickets. It would have been the absolute perfect way to spend Valentine's Day!"

"You've tried for the last three months and the concert's been sold out." Carly's voice was sympathetic.

"I even called into the radio show that was giving away tickets every morning these past two weeks, but no luck. It's not fair. I'm his biggest fan ever." Tara sounded disconsolate.

"Don't worry Tara, you still have two more days, miracles can still happen. You know you should stop mooning over a celebrity and try dating a real guy."

"That's easy for you to say your fiancé is perfect! My last boyfriend broke with me over a Facebook message and changed his relationship status to single at the same time."

"Not all guys are like that. You just need to find the right one."

"The right guy isn't going to come along before Valentine's Day and I'm going to be spending it all by my lonesome. So I might as well dream of the impossible."

"Oh! Cheer up Tara! If I didn't have plans with Michael, I would have spent it with you. Let's plan a girl's night out on Sunday, get mani-pedis and shop and then watch videos of your idol if you wish."

"You're a good friend Carly. That sounds great!"

As Carly winked and left, Tara sighed and turned back to the folder on her desk. If only a miracle would happen. She lapsed into a daydream, she was at the concert and by some stroke of fate had front row tickets right next to the stage. He would look right at her as he sang "I'm looking right at the other half of me." Then he would call her onto the stage and they would dance together...

"Barring!" the desk phone interrupted her reverie.

"Tara, I need that report ASAP." Her boss sounded impatient.

Replacing the receiver Tara sighed again. "I can't even dream in peace," she grumbled as she stared at the open report on her screen, her fingers clicking away at the keyboard with unnecessary force.

****

It can't be him. Tara's heart beat rapidly as she neared the Townsend hotel on her way back from lunch. There was a black limo outside which in itself was not unusual. Celebrities had been known to stay there on occasion. It was the Friday before the concert and it was possible that he had arrived early. "Oh! Let it be him! Please! If I can't be at the concert let me at least have that!"

As a tall figure emerged from the car, she increased her speed hoping to catch a glimpse of his face. Though she almost ran, all she saw was a dark head as it disappeared through the revolving doors. She kept walking toward the hotel but only saw two imposing men dressed in suits and sporting earwigs standing by the doors.

Feeling foolish, she continued walking. She had another block to go to reach her office building and it was a brisk February day in Michigan. Her mind started spinning another daydream. He would emerge from the hotel, see her, walk rapidly, and catch up with her. He would smile that boyish smile and...

"Arf! Arf!" the tiny but persistent bark penetrated her mind.

Looking around she spotted a little face with huge brown eyes. The puppy was frantically tugging on a leash that was tangled around a parking meter post. At first Tara thought someone had tied him up there and she looked around for an owner. The parking space next to the meter was empty. People were walking around the busy cross section, but no one stopped near the dog.

It was a chilly day, the wind was blowing, and the poor dog looked cold. She held out her hand for the puppy to sniff, and when its tail started to wag, she gently untangled the leash and picked up the puppy.

"Now who do you belong to I wonder?" she asked holding up the puppy as a lolling tongue tried to lick her face and the wagging tail created a breeze.

The puppy, a female, wriggled. It was one of the new designer breeds and was beige, with four white socks and a white tuft on the head. She guessed it to be a cockapoo. She noticed that the pink collar on the dog had a rhinestone monogram.

"JT," she read aloud. The tail wagged even more. She looked into the puppy's face and the tongue lolled even more. With its soulful eyes and cute nose she looked adorable and Tara couldn't help giving her a little kiss on the head, only to have her entire face licked in return.

"Stop! Stop it," she laughed holding her away. Then her eyes narrowed on the collar.

"JT? Justine? It couldn't be! That would be too much." Tara told herself. *What if it is?* What if it was him she'd seen at the hotel down the street and what if his puppy had run away?

Tara stood there undecided. What should she do? Passersby looked curiously at the young woman, standing in the middle of the pavement, holding the wriggling puppy 'Lion King' style.

Making up her mind she walked back to the hotel, puppy in her arms. Ignoring the curious looks that the wriggling puppy attracted, she marched up the reception desk.

"I believe she belongs to one of your guests." She held up the dog so the girl at the desk got a good view of lolling tongue and wagging tail.

"We don't allow pets in this hotel." The receptionist sounded condescending.

Her tone must have annoyed JT as much as it did Tara, as the puppy emitted some shrill barks.

"I just found her outside, she must have run away."

"Sorry no one has reported a missing puppy." The girl didn't sound at all sorry, JT seemed to think so too, and she made her opinion known.

The puppy was attracting the attention of the other guests in the hotel lobby and Tara decided to be direct.

"I think she belongs to you know..." she whispered, showing her the monogrammed collar. "He's staying here isn't he?"

"We do not give out the names of our guests and I suggest you leave before I call security."

Tara could only stare at the girl, but JT made up for her silence, letting her indignation be known.

As if by magic a security guard appeared at Tara's elbow.

"What seems to be the problem?" he said.

"Please escort this lady to the street."

As an infuriated Tara turned to leave, she heard the girl murmur sotto voce, "Can you believe it? As if such a transparent attempt, would actually work!"

Tara found herself outside holding the puppy. She was going to be late for work at this rate.

****

"You did what?" Carly's eyes were round behind her glasses and her mouth was hanging open.

"What was I supposed to do? I couldn't leave the poor thing out in the cold!"

"So where is it?"

"JT's taking a nap." Tara indicated the empty gym bag, which she had lined with her scarf. The little puppy was fast asleep.

"JT? You gave it a name?"

"No. It was on her collar. That's why I think it's his."

"What are you going to do now?"

I sent a message to his Facebook page as well as a tweet to him. I also sent an email to his fan page."

"What if it's not his? You should post some posters outside as well."

"Good idea! I'll do it before I head home this evening."

****

"Come along JT, finish your business so we can go inside. I guess you are bunking with me tonight. Looks like I may not be alone for Valentine's Day, after all." Tara gave a little tug on the leash to encourage the puppy who insisted on sniffing every inch of the driveway on the way to her door.

She had put up several posters with her cell number on it and had included Carly's cell for good measure. No one had yet called her to claim the puppy. She made a mental note to pick up some puppy food on the way home. Someone may still claim her that weekend so she wasn't going to get too attached. However watching the little fur ball scampering over the snow made her smile. It wouldn't be a bad thing if no one claimed her. She could easily make room for JT in her life.

Later that evening Tara lay on her couch with JT snuggled up next to her. Though the TV was on, her mind was in the middle of another daydream. He would contact her, and then come to her house to pick up his puppy. She would invite him in and...

"Brrring!" It was the doorbell.

JT set off a series of shrill barks that roused her out of her stupor. Heart racing she opened the door fully expecting to see her idol, with his tall frame, with the slicked back hair and blue eyes. The man she saw standing on her doorstep was slightly shorter, had wavy brown hair, and as far as she could tell his eyes looked brown. Her heart lurched in disappointment. It wasn't him!

"JT!" The man cried as JT capered about as if she had drunk five cans of an energy drink, yelping madly while tugging on the leash and jumping as high as she could on her short little legs. Her tail wagged like it had a life of its own.

"JT! Baby! I'm so glad you're okay." The man knelt on the ground and picked up the ecstatic puppy. He spoke in the same tone of voice usually used by grandmothers when talking to their grandbabies. JT responded by licking every inch of his face thoroughly with her tiny pink tongue.

"Daddy was so scared that you were hurt. Don't you ever do that again, you naughty, naughty girl." The man punctuated the words with kisses and Tara watched speechless with fascination. When he finally stood up, he flushed with embarrassment. His slightly crooked smile made his eyes crinkle in the corners.

Tara smiled back and handed over the leash. She suddenly felt very conscious of the fact that she was dressed in her oldest sweats, makeup free, with her hair in a no-nonsense ponytail.

"Thank you so much! I saw your posters and tried to call you, but you didn't answer. Your friend Carly gave me the address and suggested I should just come over. I hope you don't mind that it's so late, but I was really anxious about JT."

"It's okay." Tara glanced at her cell. It was dead. She'd forgotten to charge it after getting home. All the same she wished Carly had given her some notice that a strange man was about to show up at her doorstep. With some difficulty, she focused on the matter at hand. "Did JT run away from home?"

"No. I was bringing her in for a groom earlier today, when she saw a cat and took off. I guess I didn't have a firm grip on her leash. I've been searching for her all afternoon. I hope she wasn't too much trouble."

"No trouble at all. I'm glad to be of help. JT is just adorable!"

"My name is Josh Turner by the way and this, as you know, is JT."

"I'm Tara Venn," she shook the proffered hand. "I'm glad to help." He turned and was about to walk away when something made her ask.

"Why is she called JT?"

"My sister's a huge fan and she gave me the puppy for my birthday, name and collar were included in the gift. I'm not a fan of pink and rhinestones but don't want to hurt her feelings." He grinned abashed.

He's cute! Tara thought. "What a coincidence! I am a big fan too."

"You are?   Are you going to the concert tomorrow?"

"No such luck. I couldn't get tickets."

"That sucks! My sister bought premium tickets months ago and it's all she's been talking about." Josh gave her a sympathetic look that did nothing to cheer Tara up.

Closing the door, Tara settled back on the couch. Somehow, her living room seemed empty without JT in it. She sighed heavily. JT was going home and it was obvious that her owner adored her. That's all that mattered.

Edited by Evelyn M. Zimmer   Puppy Love: 2015

"Brrrrrrng." The strident ringing of the doorbell woke her up.

"There should be a law against ringing the doorbell before noon on a Saturday," Tara grumbled as she opened the door in her PJ's.

"Delivery for Tara Venn." The deliveryman thrust a tablet toward Tara.

Closing the door, Tara tore open the envelope. Out slid a photograph and a note.

She stared at the autographed picture and smiled. He still looked adorable. Her heart beating in anticipation, she read the handwritten note.

"Dear Tara,

I received your messages about finding Justine. I actually ended up not bringing her on tour, as she had just got spayed and needed to rest. Therefore, the puppy you found is not mine. I think it's great that you wanted to help return a lost puppy to its owner. Please show this note at the backstage door after the concert tonight. I am always glad to meet my fans especially a fellow dog lover."

His signature was scrawled on it.

He wanted to meet her backstage. Surely, he sent her tickets? Her hands shook as she turned the envelope upside down. There were a couple of backstage passes in it. No tickets! He'd assumed that she already had tickets.

Tara felt like crying. She clutched the picture and note and took them with her to bed. She had just settled back in when her cell played "... as long as I got my suit and tie..."

"Hello," Tara sounded gruffer than she intended.

"Tara? It's Josh from yesterday. JT's owner." His voice sounded nervous.

"Hi Josh." She injected some sweetness that she didn't feel into her greeting.

"You know how you said you wanted to go to the concert today? I just won two tickets on the radio. Would you like to go with me?"

Tara was dumbfounded with shock. In the ensuing silence, she could hear JT's barks over the phone.

"We could grab a bite before the concert. I know this great place in Auburn Hills." He sounded as if he had rehearsed what he was going to say and wanted to get it done fast.

Tara hesitated. She really didn't know anything about him except that he loved his dog. However, he'd seen her in her oldest sweats and still wanted to see her again. That was definitely a point in his favor. Any guy who could put up with a pink rhinestone dog collar, just to spare his sister's feelings, had to be appreciated. It would be churlish to refuse. In addition, it was Valentine's Day and she was alone. What did she have to lose?

Edited by Evelyn M. Zimmer

"Tara, are you still there? Hey listen, I know it's short notice and it is Valentine's Day and you may already have plans. Therefore, if you want to go with someone else, that's perfectly fine. You can pick up the tickets from—" his words were rushed as if he was embarrassed.

"Yes. Thanks," she interrupted him.

"What?"

"Yes. Thanks, I'll go with you."

"That's great!" The relief in his voice was audible.

"On one condition. I'm buying dinner."

"Deal! I'll pick you up at five pm."

"Thanks. That sounds great!"

"Look forward to seeing you soon."

Hanging up her cell, Tara settled back on her pillows to dream. She was backstage and suddenly their eyes met across the room...brown ones not blue. Josh Turner really was cute and his initials were JT too! Valentine's Day was not looking too bad, after all.

My Angel Jake
By Laurie Kolp

Jake became a part of our family on an impulsive whim after my husband, Pete, took a last-minute business trip to Greece without me. We'd dreamed of visiting Greece since before we married, only our plans had been put on the back burner with the birth of three children in four years. I was tired and I wanted to be on that plane with him.

The first thing I did after his departure was apply for a passport. Another opportunity wasn't going to pass me by like that again. Then I piled the kids in the car and took them to a Greek restaurant for a late lunch. It was as if a spell came over me, all rationale packed away in Pete's duffle bag.

After our not-too-well-received gyros, we stopped by the veterinarian's office to pick up a treat for our yellow lab, Sadie. I don't think I planned on getting a puppy at that point, but my kids later told me I looked like a crazy woman leaning up to the steering wheel, sly grin on my face. As we entered the screen porch and waited to proceed to the counter inside, my daughter noticed a kennel filled with adorable black and brown puppies. In no time, the four of us were huddled over the wire cage peeking in like new parents.

"Aww, they're so cute. Can we get one?" My youngest begged.

"We'll see. Let me go ask about them," I replied.

I rushed over to the counter while the kids stayed with the puppies. I was told the six-week-old puppies were orphans; their mother had died recently. After the vet tech let us hold the puppies and play with them for a while, she decided to let us take one for fifty dollars. We were established customers, so I only had to fill out a little paperwork and the puppy was ours. I never looked back.

We named him Jake. He was a German Sheppard/ Russell Terrier mix with endearing dark eyes and floppy ears. I could snuggle him in my arms and lay him on my shoulder. The kids helped me make a bed for him out of an old cardboard box from the garage. We lined it with newspaper and towels before going to sleep.

I expected to be awakened through the night by a whimpering puppy, but I did not hear a peep out of him until five-thirty the next morning. Again, the kids and I were drawn to the puppy like a magnet. We huddled over him in admiration and barely broke away long enough to eat.

As the days went by, we marveled at what a good-natured puppy Jake was. He fit right in with Sadie, who became like a mother to him. They were an odd couple but seemed connected from the start.

We sent Pete emails about the big surprise we had for him when he came home. The kids were great about not revealing the secret, but they gave my animal-loving husband enough hints for him to figure out we had gotten a kitten or puppy. When Pete arrived home and saw what a great dog Jake was, he rejoiced in our decision.

Jake quickly became my dog. I stayed at home while the kids were in school and Pete was at work, so Jake and I spent a lot of time together. He claimed a chair behind my computer as his and sat there while I wrote.

I had a good friend, Anna, who came over a lot. She called him "Jake-ee-poo" and loved him as much as I did. In fact, she even gave him baths just because she felt like it.

That same friend committed suicide one day out of the blue. Devastation knocked me into a deep depression. I blamed myself for not having seen the signs while mourning the loss of Anna. I spent a lot of time crying, and Jake sat by my side through it all. In fact, Jake comforted me with his presence.

One day I was overwrought with emotion. I plopped in a chair by the window, which was next to his, and bawled my eyes out. It was one of those unrelenting crying spells with gasps for air and cries for help. I just wanted to know why God sent this friend to me and then took her away so fast.

I had shied away from women for several years after a falling out with a social climber, my home a refuge as I felt like a woman scorned by all society in the small town where I live. I compared myself to Hester in The Scarlet Letter wearing a red letter on my forehead; only my letter was L for Loser. This woman, who eventually moved away, made my life miserable through her lies and petty antics. For years, I kept myself sheltered from that kind of hurt.

That is until Anna came into my life. In the few short months we knew each other, she boosted my confidence and restored my faith in friendship; all while unbeknownst to me, she was dying on the inside. If only I'd been more perceptive.

All of this ran through my mind that day like a never-ending train that goes on and on and on, my tears the exhaust. All of the sudden, I remember feeling a cold, wet nose on my arm nudging me. I looked up and there was Jake with a concerned look in his eyes. He sat by my side like a sentinel, and for some reason, the urge to cry lifted. He jumped up onto the table by my chair and got as close as he could without getting too close. He then placed his chin on my shoulder. I calmed down almost immediately.

What a friend I had in Jake, and still do today. He loves me unconditionally and is always by my side. At night, he tells me when he wants to get in his kennel and go to bed by coming up and nudging me with his wet nose like he did that day seven years ago. He can be very persistent! I just know that's what he wants. And when he needs to go outside, he runs back and forth from the door to wherever I am. Sometimes he stares at his food until I say, "Eat, Jake." Only then will he start to eat.

My family has truly been blessed with a pet angel. Jake has been by our side and seen us through hurricanes, death and other trying circumstances. He loves us unconditionally and lightens our load through this journey called life.

Photo Provided by Laurie Kolp

Of Possums and Poetry

By Stephanie Madan

I thought it was my destiny to own Natalie, my neighbor's black standard poodle. If not her, her clone. Natalie is refined. So refined that at times, she is forced to self-medicate by reciting T S Eliot cat poems to herself. This occurs mainly when boisterous conversations are initiated by other dogs. I do not judge her any the less superior. Natalie is elegant. I nominate her the Grace Kelly of dogs.

It is my fate to own Amanda, our Westie. This is a dog closely associated with my sociable spouse Paul finishing a third glass of Pouilly-Fuissé at a charity event, just as the live-auction puppy was introduced. Amanda is cheerful and self-confident, but any intimations of elegance and refinement are well-concealed.

One night I declined to join Paul at a cocktail party honoring a new automobile model. I am not about to put on a cocktail dress to honor a car. I mocked Paul for being seduced by expensive cars and the prospect of models in miniscule dresses lounging on them. How he found that more appealing than spaghetti casserole and a healthy salad at home is baffling. He ignored my jeers with the air of a man anticipating a pleasant superficial evening with no regret, and so it happened I arrived home alone.

I opened the door. Amanda, poised on the other side, streaked into the garden while I instructed her to sit. My standing as pack leader is one she often ignores. Thus, neither of us was surprised by this. We were surprised, however, that she proceeded to corner a possum within seconds.

Westies are bred to trap badgers in their dens, providing location-identifying barks until the owner arrives. Amanda entered into the spirit of things with ecstatic announcements of her skill that took barking to another level.

Where was Paul when needed? Not answering his phone, that's where. No doubt models were already popping hors d'oeuvres into his mouth while the sales manager assured him he, among all men, deserved to own the first new model in the land. That, as I was confronting Nature.

I called my neighbor James who owns schnauzers and knows things. It was bad luck that James was attending a meeting in Bakersfield and that the things he knows are not about possums. He guessed I must wade in and grab Amanda.

First, I was wearing stiletto ankle boots – stylish, but not crafted with actual walking in mind. I am an uncoordinated individual and must concentrate to negotiate a doorway without bouncing off one side or the other. Wearing stiletto boots was more than a fashion statement, it was an act of courage.

Second, it is my highest truth that a two-foot possum transforms into a six-foot hissing monster when trapped by a short, barking white dog. Amanda remained fearless and engaged full throttle on that barking part even so. I saw the future: She would soon be mauled by a possum that had expected to be staring death in the face and come to realize its situation wasn't that dire.

Reader, I saved her. In my stiletto ankle boots, I wobbled into the battle, not without encountering bushes that wished me ill. I hauled an outraged Amanda out of harm's way, promptly dropped her and managed a body block to prevent her from re-engaging. We retreated to the house where I suffered baleful glares that not even the offering of a raw chicken wing could soften.

There's a moral lurking somewhere. I hate the fact that it may be when in doubt about accepting an invitation to honor a car, just do it.

I suppose something about destiny and poodles would also be appropriate. How will I ever know whether Natalie is my destiny or just my idea of my destiny? Natalie recites poetry. Amanda yodels at possums. I rescue Amanda from monsters. The answer lies in there somewhere.

Olga, Mama and Mugsey

By Robert Iulo

The neighborhood was known as Fulton Ferry although the ferry stopped running when the bridge was built a hundred years before. I lived in a loft there, under the Brooklyn Bridge and just across the street from the East River. Most of my space was used as a studio where I did portfolios for models and entertainers and any other photography jobs that came my way.

Back then, in the seventies, what later became known as DUMBO was a gritty waterfront district. The Brooklyn piers were still active and loud with longshoreman and trucks lining up, waiting to load and unload and there was a metal recycling facility just about where the River Café would eventually open. Most of the buildings were run-down warehouses and small factories built in the nineteenth century and the people living there were musicians and artists in illegal lofts like I was. The whole area was buzzing with activity during the day but quiet at night and on weekends. Chances were that anyone you saw on the street at those times lived there, and since so few of us did live there we all got to know one another. We were like pioneers staking our claim on an unsettled corner of Brooklyn.

Olga Bloom was one of my neighbors. She lived on an old coffee barge. She got it for a song, refurbished its interior with recycled and donated materials and had it towed to a dilapidated pier at the foot of Fulton Street. A small section of her barge was reserved for living space leaving the rest for her chamber music recitals. Sometimes at night I would go to the pier to look at the river and the downtown Manhattan skyline. I could hear, through the steel walls of the barge, Olga playing her violin.

She had a scruffy, but cute dog named Mama, who would come out to play when someone was on the pier. One night Mama wasn't there, but another dog was. He looked something like a German Sheppard but not quite and with no collar I figured he was a stray. He poked my hand with his snout a few times until I got the message and scratched his ears. It didn't end there because he followed me across the street to the door of my building and looked at me sadly as I started to go in.

I supposed it wouldn't hurt if I took him home for some fresh water and scrounged up something for him to eat. I had half of a chicken cutlet sandwich in the fridge and supplemented that with Wheaties and milk. He was well behaved and ate politely although clearly very hungry. When he finished eating, he circled my welcome mat a few times then lay down and went to sleep. Seeing that, I decided to let him spend the night and would send him on his way in the morning.

I awoke the next day with him standing beside my bed nudging me with his wet nose. It was time to let him go, but I knew I couldn't just put him back out on his own. I walked him and then started calling friends to see if any of them wanted a dog. I gave him a big build up and all I got in return were a few who said, "Let me think about it." A bath would make him more appealing, I thought, so I got him into the tub. He must have been on the street for a long time. He was filthy but after a few washes, rinses and repeats, he looked good enough for the Westminster Dog Show. He felt better too and seemed really happy to be clean, wildly running from one end of my loft to the other, jumping and chasing his tail. After he had settled down, I took him shopping. We got a leash, collar, and enough dog food for the few days I'd have to wait to see if any of my friends wanted him. Then I thought of Olga. She had plenty of room and already had one dog so maybe she'd like another.

We went down to the pier and found Olga on deck doing some gardening.

She noticed him immediately and said, "Hey, when did you get a dog?"

"He's a stray I found here last night. He followed me home and ..." then I went on about what a great dog he was.

As I was making my pitch, Mama came out and she and Mugsey started to play.

I took advantage of this and asked, "Don't you think he'd be a perfect companion for Mama? Look at how well they get along."

"No thanks," Olga replied, "One is enough."

As she was petting him, she said, "So what did you name him?"

"I didn't name him. He's not my dog."

"Well, I think he's your dog, at least for a little while. He needs a name."

We were looking him over trying to come up with something suggested by his appearance when Olga said, "I guess he's kind of a street urchin so how about Mugsey? You remember, one of the East Side Kids from the old movies?"

I had been resisting naming him but I couldn't resist 'Mugsey.' It suited him perfectly. So now I had a dog, at least for a little while, named Mugsey.

When none of my friends who had to "think about it," came through, I decided Mugsey would be my dog permanently. Living with him became a real adventure. He couldn't keep from chasing garbage trucks and snapping at their rear tires. He loved to sniff the cinnamon residue on the vent outside a spice grinding factory just make himself sneeze.

Whenever I had him out at night, he'd track down a waterfront rat. The first time it took some sparring before Mugsey got the upper hand. After that, when he got better at it, there'd be a brief standoff ending with him grabbing the rat by the back of the neck and killing it with a quick shake. Then he'd proudly come back to me for a "good boy" and pat on the head.

He was so friendly and entertaining that my customers all liked him. I'd often set up shots of elegantly dressed models against rough industrial backgrounds in the local streets and truck chasing, cinnamon sniffing, rat killing Mugsey would accompany us. His friend Mama would sometimes come along too.

As I was photographing a dancer in a graceful pose against a rugged masonry wall, her eyes widened and her dramatic expression gave way to a smile as she pointed to what was happening behind me. Mugsey and Mama were mating and there wasn't anything I could do to stop them. It never occurred to me that something like that would happen. I didn't know how old Mama was, but I thought of her as elderly. She had gray whiskers and with a name like Mama I imagined her as being senior to Mugsey and not sexually appealing to him. I was mistaken. They finally ended their very long embrace, rolled around on their backs, stretched a bit and then continued playing as if nothing had happened. The look on that dancer's face for those remaining photos could never be duplicated.

Afraid she'd think I should have known better and paid more attention to Mama and Mugsey when they were with me, I dreaded having to face Olga and tell her what happened. But she took it calmly and said she thought Mama was probably too old to get pregnant even if she did have sex.

She said, "Let's not worry about it and see what happens."

I was embarrassed and felt guilty about the whole thing but put at ease by Olga being so calm and understanding. She was wrong about Mama. About eight weeks later Olga asked me to come on board to show me something in her closet. Mama must have been a lot younger than we thought because, amidst a pile of shoes, she was nursing six pups, all looking an awful lot like their father. I had already made a visit to the vet with Mugsey for a serious discussion about family planning and then to help with child support I supplied Olga with puppy chow until all six were adopted.

Not long after that, as the area became more popular, I had to move out of my loft because of a rent increase I couldn't afford. I gave up photography and decided to get a real job and a real apartment; unfortunately it was one that didn't allow dogs. By then a nearby warehouse had been converted into luxurious legal apartments and a young couple who moved in agreed to take Mugsey. I knew I'd miss him but was glad he wouldn't have to leave his home on the waterfront where he could catch rats, sniff cinnamon and hang out with his old girlfriend Mama.

Pet Peeves

By Gary Beck

Sometimes I don't understand why I didn't get rid of Pard when he was a puppy. Now he had become an inseparable part of my life. Three walks a day at Thompkins Square Park. Two meals a day. Doggie vitamins. Doggie treats. Biscuits. Endless poaching on my leftovers. Fortunately so far, only a few visits to the veterinarian, the dreaded and expensive monster who Pard loathed. As if by ESP, Pard knew when we were getting ready to go to the vet. First his ears would droop, then he'd hide although there wasn't much concealment in our tiny east village apartment. When I finally trapped him, he would manage to get away each time that I tried to put on his collar. At last, with collar and leash in place, I'd have to drag him out the door. How did the infernal mutt know where we were going? Then the ordeal of dragging him through the streets. The second time we went through this exasperating ritual I yelled at him, something I never did before. A righteous old lady materialized as if by magic and whomped me with her umbrella, admonishing me for 'pet abuse'. People stared at me like I was the pet executioner at the S.P.C.A. Pard and I slunk off, tails between our legs, albeit for entirely different reasons.

When we finally reached the vet, Pard would give me the most anguished look of betrayal imaginable. His eyes contained such pathos that I could only wish my acting students at Gotham University School of the Arts could emulate this exponent of the art of silent acting. His ears of dejection, an asset that my students would have to do without, although they needed them more than my expressive dog, were truly heart rendering. I experienced the peculiar frustrations of the dog owner, doing something for the good of the pet that wasn't appreciated. I had tried several times to explain to Pard that the visit to the vet was necessary, to no avail. So on the infrequent occasions when Pard was destined to suffer at the hands of Dr. Mengele's heir, I steeled my resolution and took him, regardless of his woe, for shots or other torments.

I learned a lot about myself from taking care of a dog. I realized that I certainly wasn't ready for the responsibility of children. It was traumatic enough taking a dog to the vet, so I could only imagine how a parent would feel, rushing a stricken child to the hospital. However, I also noticed that I was developing a little bit of patience. Granted, I still had a big mouth that sounded off too quickly, with an acerbic wit that offended most people, but there were occasions, albeit infrequent, when I actually suppressed biting comments that would have wounded my students. It wasn't that I thought of them as dumb beasts to be protected, well, perhaps I privately ascribed to that theory, but they were my charges, even though they weren't an endangered species. In fact, I believe we could probably do without a few million students if we could only replace them with old fashioned handy people: electricians, plumbers, and mechanics with blue collar skills that we no longer respect in our on-line society.

Well, I guess that's enough meaningless griping. The truth be known, I bonded with Pard a while ago and he was an integral part of my life. I talked to him more than to my friends and he was probably more empathetic. I never feared a break-in, which was especially reassuring, since my landlord was eager to get rid of me and I wouldn't put it past him to arrange a destructive burglary. I also never worried about walking Pard late at night, because he was very protective and wouldn't let anyone suspicious approach me without growling menacingly. I had grown fond of him. Well, that's an understatement. I loved him without reservation, something I couldn't say about anyone else in this life. I didn't question how he mastered the look of total adoration that could only be learned in doggie acting 101.

Now that I was a dog owner, I had become very aware of how other people treated their dogs. I wasn't particularly tolerant of the abusive behavior that people inflicted on their devoted pets: yanking them harshly for not anticipating the master's intentions; smacking, kicking, and cursing the confused beast who only wanted to please. This attitude caused me to make negative remarks to certain dog owners, further alienating me from the regular dog walkers, who already considered me a procurer for an oversexed predator dog. My previous stalking of female dogs for Pard was bad enough, but somehow the Tompkins Square Park dog walkers had found out that I was the publisher of the short-lived 'Doggie Tribune', which I had started to find a sex partner for Pard. Someone must have seen me dropping off copies of the newsletter in the neighborhood and spread the word. Instead of a landmark trial that Peter Zenger would have admired, I was condemned by rumor and gossip. I wasn't deluded enough to think that this was a constitutional issue, but it would have been nice to have an opportunity to defend myself.

The only consequences of my actions on behalf of Pard's sex life so far were neglect and scorn, but I couldn't help wondering why no one was amused by my witty writing in the 'Doggie Tribune.' Perhaps I wasn't as clever as I thought. I could brood about my various failures if I chose, or I could try to bring some order out of the chaos that swirled around me. This was an opportunity to cherish the positive elements in my life. I had a good job, a nice apartment and a faithful dog. Spring would be here soon, which would allow me to do my silent clown show again and test the new material for my planned one man show. So I didn't have a girlfriend at the moment. That could change. Why I could turn a corner, bump into an exciting beauty and a random event would bring us together. Meanwhile, I made a mental note not to stare at the nubiles in my acting class. That was one complication I certainly didn't need. Oh, but some of the corn fed sirens could tempt a man of lesser willpower or a dumber one. I repeated a mantra several times: 'Don't think about them.' 'Don't think about them.' 'Don't think about them.'

Of course, the next time I was in class I promptly forgot my resolution and eyeballed several of the more delectable morsels. Fortunately for me, before eye contact was established and recognition signals exchanged, I managed to clamp down on my restless libido and resume the bland classroom demeanor that allowed me to avoid entangling alliances. I garnered a few puzzled expressions, but none significant enough to stimulate a request for a private conference. Whew. I almost had to bite the bullet, whatever that means. I invoked self-control just in time to avert calamity. Nothing good could result from a dalliance with a student. If discovered, I would be discharged immediately, subjected to public contumely if I had a public, and possibly degraded in the media, which would cause my family no end of humiliation. And even if there were no negative consequences, what could I hope for from this unnatural teacher/student relationship? Anything more than enthusiastic sex? Improbable, since the student was an inexperienced girl.

So I formed a new resolve to put temptation behind me and find a suitable girlfriend. Let the rapidly expanding lesbian population at Gotham U. sneak up on the naïve girl students and lead them into whatever. Yet it was uncanny how a man's sexual need was so easily sensed by women, who were never as urgent. This peculiar difference in attitudes or needs had made me almost as horny as my lustful mutt, and just as unsuccessful socially. But I wasn't in the mood for internal debates about hormonal differences, so I decided to go to the Tompkins Square library after class and do some research in theater production. I made a mental note to check out some of the east village internet cafés after the library closed. These days, you never knew who you'd find on-line. While two of my students tepidly droned on making the incendiary passion of Romeo and Juliet into a middle-class date, I drifted into a fantasy about spotting an exotic woman at a café. Our eye contact flared into instant desire. I was boldly approaching her, when the silence from the mutilators of Shakespeare brought me back to the room. I made some sedative comments, dismissed the class and fled to the library of refuge.

I started browsing the web and became hopelessly trapped on the pages of one of those monstrous hunting and fishing sites that peddled everything imaginable for the outdoorsman. I kept scrolling through an endless collection of doggie beds, couches and boxes that came in a vast array of shapes, sizes and colors, all modeled by happy dogs. I wanted to get one for Pard to console him for his lack of a sex life, but I couldn't decide between the ultra hi-tech hyper-thermal bed and the deluxe foam reclining sofa. I couldn't help wondering what kind of society needed almost as many beds for dogs as there were for people. Perhaps I could train Pard to use my credit cards to save me from the stress of decision-making. While I wrestled the demon of bed choice, I browsed the section of doggie boots. It was as congested as beds. I particularly favored the nifty styles in neoprene and suede. I finally gave up on a purchase, hoping Pard would never know and took a break.

The library was crowded with the usual assortment of the mentally active senior citizens who would rather read than obliterate themselves in TV, scruffy students, the odiferous homeless, pretentious researchers and horny hopefuls like me. Two tables down a gorgeous redhead was intent on a laptop. Every seat was taken at her table, so there was no way to move closer. I stared longingly at her pale, freckled face, pert nose, and lickable lips, framed by her shimmering hair. Instant lust possessed me and I sent her urgent ESP messages of desire that were ignored. I didn't know if I was transmitting poorly, or if she had her mind shield up, but she wasn't receiving anything. My eyeballs began to ache from optically devouring her and I let my gaze wander around the room. At least three other cavaliers were preening and displaying, futilely trying to catch her eye, so I went back to the complications of theater production. I plowed through page after page of material for Broadway and regional theaters that had enormous budgets. I couldn't find anything that applied to small budget production and gave up in disgust. I tried again to reach the dazzling redhead with my penetrating look, but was unsuccessful. I looked around the room in search of another attractive female, but the most eligible was over sixty-five, with her head buried in a crocheting magazine. I called it a day and went home to take faithful Pard for his evening walk.

By the time we got to the park, it was rush hour, but still a bit early for most of the regular dog walkers. Pard romped, chased squirrels, barked at crows and I didn't have any confrontations with the locals, which was a pleasant change. When the usual hasslers began to arrive, I called Pard, who reluctantly obeyed. After all, the poor mutt was cooped up in the house all day, while I was out somewhere, having a blast without him. I exited the park at Avenue A and slowly walked south, checking out the cafés. I noted one or two for a follow-up visit while carefully monitoring Pard to make sure he didn't get us into trouble. In warm weather, he would try to snatch food from the tables of outdoor cafés, and he was so quick and sneaky that he frequently succeeded. When he got caught, I would apologize profusely and rebuke him for the benefit of the indignant diner. He would look woeful and invariably earn forgiveness.

I always had to be alert when we were outdoors because he constantly looked for plump, overfed pedigreed pooches that he could nip. Nothing delighted him more than the outraged squeals of a pampered victim and doting master. If you ever saw a dog laugh, you'd appreciate Pard's moments of hilarity. He moaned, snuffled, snorted, hopped around and actually chortled with delight. My apologies were never acceptable and I slunk off to the usual threats of police, dogcatcher, and vengeful boyfriend. Despite all the tensions in these canine incidents, I must confess Pard amused me.

He was such a mischievous swashbuckler that I couldn't get angry at him. I almost envied his devil-may-care attitude. I was a little shy and reluctant to risk rejection. He plunged in regardless of consequences. I guess it was the lack of a sexual and social life that led to my identification with doggie activities.

I had spaghetti and meatballs for dinner and Pard consumed his share, a portion as large as mine. The mutt even gobbled down a piece of garlic bread. Well, at least I wasn't dining alone. Afterward, I sat down to read and became completely absorbed in a Restoration comedy by Aphra Behn, the first professional woman playwright. The 'Emperor of the Moon' was a silly farce about a foolish doctor who believed there was a superior civilization on the moon. While the doctor watched the moon through his primitive telescope, his irreverent servants schemed to thwart the marriage of his daughter to a rich old man. I just got to the scene where the servants pretended to descend from the moon, when Pard reminded me that it was time for the late night walk by bringing me his leash. Well, another escape from frustrating reality shattered. I may not have been able to change anything in my life by complaining about it, but at least these days I got a lot more exercise dog walking.

Philosophy
Of Dogs

By Stephanie Madan

Margaritas were under construction by Althea's parents and Papa, her grandfather, in his kitchen. Althea, age almost-five, remained perched on the sofa in the living room, awaiting cherry Kool-Aid and eyeing Papa's recliner, with its five angle settings and its vibrating heating pad with three heat settings, a chair she had been discouraged from approaching.

She knew to be wary of BZ, short for Beelzebub, Papa's black and tan dachshund. BZ guarded his position on Papa's lap in the recliner with ferocity. However, BZ had left the room. Althea found it impossible to ignore this development.

BZ was missing because he had followed the grownups into the kitchen toward BZ's bliss, a clear view of Papa's blender blades. The blades of Papa's blender, as they sliced through ice and tequila and Cointreau, as they, with professional nonchalance eviscerated key limes, even the peels, provoked in BZ a peculiar elation that excited in him a quiver quite delightful.

As his quivering delightful commenced, Althea was still seated on the sofa in the living room, debating whether or not she wished to be a good child. This phase was soon over.

BZ, troubled by an inchoate uneasiness, interrupted his blender-induced rapture that day. He padded on stubby, still-exhilarated legs toward the living room and, from the hall, spied Althea invading his consecrated province. She was seated in Papa's recliner, his recliner, humming a little hum as she tested its possibilities.

Here was a transgression inexcusable within BZ's world-view. Although he was familiar with Cicero's ancient warning that Nature abhors annihilation, fundamental etiquette had been breached. He growled and bared his teeth as he launched his outraged self toward her. Althea acknowledged his intent by wetting her pants like a baby on the recliner, angle setting three, and on the vibrating heating pad, heat setting one, and had to be rescued from a truly humiliating situation.

****

Althea, months later and now age five-and-a-half, found herself recalling The Recliner Incident when her parents brought home a five-month-old terrier she had not requested. She named him Skippy the Petty Dog since she assumed her parents would dominate his life. Here was a dog she would pet upon occasion under controlled circumstances. No, her parents informed her, Skippy was hers.

Skippy expended substantial energy during that introductory period emitting ecstatic barks interspersed with joy-jumping. Althea, uneasy, made no moves at all. Nevertheless, an optimist and philosopher by nature, Skippy immediately sensed he and Althea enjoyed that marriage of true minds that admits no impediment, no boundaries. Thus, an hour after they were introduced he captured a sociable bite of the peanut butter and banana sandwich she sat eating on a backdoor step, the same sandwich she, to his shock, flung away. Skippy rushed over to finish it, avoiding waste being among his core values. Althea ran inside, sobbing for protection.

Althea soon returned, embracing a nascent philosophy, one tolerant of pragmatism. Her mother had promised her a quarter if she would stay outside fifteen minutes.

Situated on the bottom step of the three leading up to the kitchen, Althea observed Skippy playing at the far end of the yard. Her long ponytail spilled onto the step above. Meanwhile, engaged in shaking something newly dead, Skippy spied her and galloped her way. He greeted her by depositing a partially chewed lizard on her lap, then pouncing on her ponytail, making it true she had dog toes walking on her hair. She was allowed to retreat.

Day two, Althea, having renegotiated the quarter as earned if she walked the yard's perimeter, survived Skippy's improvised welcome of licking all ten toes peeking out of her new sandals, licks he felt appropriate considering their spiritual connection. Having borne this greeting, Althea proceeded to walk. Her tense excursion was almost complete when she stepped into a mound of squishy stuff that seeped in between her toes. Fresh Skippy poop. Althea announced this by shrieking, falling to the ground under the clothes line and parting ways with her breakfast Cheerios. Skippy found this peculiar but was happy enough to do a great lot of smelling and licking before Althea's mother appeared.

It was the next day and Skippy remained philosophical. As he barked his love for her from the back window of the car taking him far away, Skippy recalled a line or two from a Winnie the Pooh story he liked very much, "'We'll be Friends Forever, won't we, Pooh?' asked Piglet. 'Even longer,' Pooh answered."

Puppy Love
By Evelyn M. Zimmer

Dear Reader, allow me to fill you in on the progression that turned a staunchly anti-dog human into a true dog lover. When it comes down to it, it's all my brother's fault. Thanks a lot baby brother! This is just another reason why you are one of my very favorite humans.

Enter Mason

Photo Provided by Evelyn M. Zimmer

"Mason is a fun little puppy, but I still think you should have called him 'Punt', and seriously, a white dog? Really? I can't believe you got a dog at all, you caved so quickly!" I remember laughing at my baby brother when I was visiting him nearly five years ago at Thanksgiving. You see we never had pets when we were growing up. My brother made a good show of not liking the dog and saying Mason wasn't a real dog because he wasn't a Sheppard. My brother claims he only caved in because his daughter, my darling niece, needed this dog to preserve her psyche. Mason has turned out to be a delightfully loyal and loving dog for the family. Even my nephew loves him. Somehow, however, Mason ended up being my sister-in-laws dog when all was said and done. They have a special bond. She feeds him and takes him to the groomer, and he adores her every footstep.

Evidently he is a Multi–Doodle. They tell me that means he is half Maltese and half Toy-Poodle. In my world, that means, hypo-allergenic, non-shedding, and will never be over seventeen pounds. My sister-in-law did a thorough job of researching breeders and found one down south when they were ready. This meant flying the dog to Minnesota. If I remember correctly, I wasn't very understanding back then and thought this a foolish waste of money. If I only knew then what I know now.

My next exposure to Mason was the following year at my darling nieces dance recital which happened to feature my darling baby brother as well. I went out there in June that year. Since they live in Minnesota and I live in Michigan, Facebook, and the occasional text message was my only news of the puppy.

It didn't take long for Mason to decide that I was family too as he sat on the arm of the chair I favored the whole time I was there, very cat-like. He earned bonus points for not being a yappy, lick-y, jumpy dog.

This started a kernel of need in the exceptionally deep recesses of my mind, easy to forget, yet still nagging. You see a void had begun in my soul as my children had the audacity to grow up and move out. My husband is a police officer and works staggered hours. Where was I going to expend all this left over mothering? Need I say more?

****

Enter Macy

Photo Provided by Evelyn M. Zimmer

"What does hypo-allergenic really mean? I didn't know that some dogs didn't shed, I mean, I guess I *knew* because my brother's dog is that way too. But really no shedding? It seems like every dog I come across either sniffs my crotch, jumps on me with muddy paws or leaves me fur covered." My best friend assured me that dear little Macy not only wouldn't jump on me, but also she couldn't reach my crotch if she wanted to and would definitely not leave me fur covered. I continued with what I thought was a sage observation, "And I like that Macy isn't a yappy little mutt."

I joked with my best friend when her daughter shipped her dog back to her to take care of until she was done with college. "So much for an empty nest..." You see, I really was clueless.

Macy is a pretty liver and white purebred Shih-Tzu with very lovely manners. She is adorably laid back and calm. Just what I needed to water that kernel in the back of my mind. Over the next couple of years, with close proximity to her charms, I was losing the anti-dog edge and learning to enjoy the pleasure of what a dog can bring to a person.

The day I acknowledged to myself that I really wanted a dog, and could learn to do it, meaning learn how to care for one, was when Macy did the most amazing thing.

She rang the bell that hung from my best friends' front door. She needed to go out to potty. No yapping or any other in-your-face behavior. She patiently waited until her human, aka my best friend, got her shoes on and then reached for the collar and leash. I was amazed. "How long did it take you to teach her that?" I asked. I wish I could say I remembered her answer, but I was fantasizing about what my future puppy would look like and how I was going to convince my husband that I hadn't lost my mind.

Shortly after that, I began dog sitting Macy when her humans were out of town.

****

The Search Begins

Being out of work during that juncture of my life left me with way too much time to search the internet. I started by Googling non-shedding dogs. Then I started to narrow the search by size, I was sure I wanted a small lap-dog. Then I began looking at color, a color that matched the palate of my home. I remember thinking that I couldn't possibly have a dog that clashed with my earth toned environment. I felt like it would set my nerves on edge. Don't judge me. I was going to have to live with this animal in my non-pet home for the next fifteen years or so. Also, I needed a face I wasn't going to get sick of. I settled on a Toy-Poodle/King Cavalier mix called a Cava-poo. In my naiveté, I swear that I approached this entire process of finding my perfect dog as if I was placing a special order for furniture. Even I shake my head at my pre-puppy ignorance.

During this frantic search, I discovered what puppy mills were, the evils they wrought and how they disguised themselves as breeders. I also discovered that there were no nearby legitimate breeders in the state of Michigan and if I were really dead set on this particular breed, I would have to go out of state to get one. With prices reaching upwards of two thousand dollars just for the puppy, not to mention the cost of flying it to Michigan, I began to re-think this situation. Did I mention I was unemployed at the time?

This entire time my husband patiently rolled his eyes and kept saying, "Umm, No." Which was funny because he adores every dog we meet, you see he grew up with small horses, I mean Great Danes.

****

Enter the Pet Shop Dog,
aka Freckles

As time marched on, as it always does, I kept up a not so secret search for the perfect dog on the internet. I admit I had a close call at the local mall when my husband and I passed by the pet shop and stopped in "just to look honey, I want to see what the different types look like."

I swear that is what I said, and again he rolled his eyes saying, "Riiiight." He may have also said "My ass," but I prefer not to remember that too closely.

The staff was friendly and let us look around and I began to ask if they ever got in Cava-poo's in the particular color choice I wanted and, of course, there was a waiting list. Then I began to tell the sales girl what I was looking for in a dog. Very specifically. She humored me as we looked at the Shih-poo, Bish-poo's, and other poo mixes, Cava-Tzu, Cava-chon as well as a number of other weird scientifically matched breeds they had there that day. I kept saying to my husband that I didn't want an solid white dog that had sad, weepy eyes, it'd be depressing. He may have rolled his eyes again. But instead he said "Oh, cool, look at this miniature Australian Sheppard," and even sillier comments like "aww, look at this guy, he'd be great," as he pointed out an English Bulldog.

"Babe, smaller, think smaller, and non-shedding. And non-drooling." I cocked an eyebrow in reproof and continued on speaking to the sales clerk, "Why does the fur under their eyes look so wet?" She explained that I'd have to learn to live with it and that they sold a 'wipe' that I could administer daily to help with the stains and that the stains under the eyes were genetic.

I don't think my comment back was flattering. I must admit that the thought of having to clean my dog's face every day made me shudder. Maybe I wasn't cut out for a dog, after all.

As my husband was ogling a Jack Russell Terrier, I saw a Fruggle. Giggling I asked the clerk how they came up with that name, "Please don't tell me that's a cross between a frog and pug." She wasn't amused.

At last we came upon a white and liver Cocker-poo. Success! My hopes soared, only to find out she was a female. Her face was adorable with no discernable nasty weepy tear stains and her face was speckled as if she had freckles. Not one to go down without a fight, I asked if we could spend time with her. The clerk of course agreed and we spent about half an hour in a little cubicle where she proceeded to love all over my husband who was trying to talk sense into me while attempting to ignore, meaning not get attached to the puppy. The puppy was ignoring me completely. I took a selfie of Freckles and myself and sent it to my best friend who promptly texted my husband and said, "Stop Her. *Now.*" I'm pretty sure that is what she texted anyway. Then my husband took a picture of me with the dog and he Facebooked it. I believe he was trying to get help in stopping me in my madness.

Photo Provided by Evelyn M. Zimmer

As I slowly came to my senses, I tried to assure my husband that I had not, in fact, lost my mind. That of course I was not going to get *that* dog, she was a girl, not the right color, was going to be bigger than I wanted and cost three times what I was willing to spend. He responded with "ah huh."

We left poor Freckles at the pet store and went to lunch. My goal of course was to talk my husband into letting me have my way. He put up convincing arguments of why the timing was bad and how I was 'not ready' for the responsibilities of a puppy. I believed my qualifications spoke for themselves. You see, I raised two successful boys into responsible citizens. How hard could a dog be after that? In the end, I hated that he was right, and I believe that I came around to agreeing that that dog wasn't for me, gracefully. At least that's what I tell myself.

After lunch, we had to pass by the pet shop to leave the mall. Freckles had been adopted already. Guess hubby was right, not my dog.

****

Enter Chanook

More time passes and while I haven't given up on the idea of a dog, I put it on the back burner where it continued to germinate. I whiled away the time by doing internet research on how to be a good doggie mom with articles on how to crate train for potty training, vaccination schedules, food types and what not to feed your dog. Obedience training philosophies and other such useful information I also diligently tried to learn via the internet.

Good news finally comes our way and I get the job of a lifetime as an editor. My boss ran her company from her home. She has two enormous dogs, a Golden Retriever, and a Boxer mix. Granted these are not huge dogs, but to me they most certainly were! These gentle giants did help to alleviate my fear of big dogs, they even helped teach me about tolerance, which was all on their part, by the way. They tolerated me. Which taught me to be less fearful. They greet me loudly and fondly whenever I work at my boss's office, and I'm grateful they do not sniff nor jump.

Shortly after that, I had an opportunity to visit my oldest son in San Antonio. My husband couldn't get the time off of work, so I went down alone. My youngest son and my husband had been cracking jokes about how funny it would be to watch me deal with that Husky that our eldest owned. They were still convinced I was never going to be a dog 'person'. They were ever so kind when they'd remind me, "You know, you'll have to take the dog out when he's at work," and other helpful things like "You know the dog sheds right?" Those two are always so funny.

Secretly, the thought of this originally terrified me. When I arrived in San Antonio, my oldest picked me up at the airport and on the way back to his new home I asked him a couple of questions about Chanook. "He stays in the cage right? I mean, that's what he does when you're at work. I don't want to disrupt his routine."

"Mom, you'll be fine. Chanook is a good boy. And it's a crate, not a cage." He just smiled at me and I thought to myself that there couldn't be a better test of whether I'd ever be a dog person or not. Since my son had to work while I was there, I knew that I would be spending my days with a white shedding Husky that would probably knock me down and jump all over me. I confess, I was nervous.

The first thing we did, when we got to my son's new house, was to let the dog out. He was in his crate. He yowled a happy greeting and thumped his tail vigorously as my son approached the beast. Okay, he's not a beast, but my fear level was on overdrive. Expecting to be mauled, I steeled myself as my son reached for the crate handle to open it up.

"Stay. Good boy," my son said with a hand gesture to the dog. The dog stayed put. He cocked his head, but he stayed put. My son looked at me and grinned. He was proud of his puppy. "Watch this," he said to me as he walked away and went to the front door. Chanook was still 'staying' inside his open crate. When my son opened the front door, he said, "Okay, outside."

Chanook bolted like he was on fire, gave me a glance as he went by, but he had a goal in mind. Outside he went.

"Stop him! He'll run into the road! He's not on a leash!" I yelled at my son.

"Mom, relax, Chanook has this."

I ran outside to see that Chanook did indeed 'have this'. He circled the tree in the front yard, did his business and sniffed around the grass and did a little 'parameter check' and trotted back to my son and looked at me. I swear it looked as if he was saying "So Dad, is this Grandma?" My son scratched his ears and petted him a little, praising him. "See Mom, he knows what to do."

"How do you keep him from going into the road? What if he bolts after a kid on a bike or car or something?" I asked in ignorance.

"Because I trained him." There was such pride in my son's voice, it made me smile. I wasn't convinced, but I wasn't going to argue.

He grabbed hold of Chanook's collar and said, "Well, come on over and meet your grandson!" We laughed as I came closer and I gave Chanook my hand to sniff, then slowly I patted him on the back of his neck and down his back. I was rewarded with about a half pound of fur. But it was soft fur.

He never jumped on me, but he did bark when he needed something. Chanook seemed to know that I was family and belonged there. I decided to act as if inside I wasn't scared of getting bit. He seemed to know that I needed to be approached slowly. After all, I was the scared one, not him.

My son was proud of my efforts to turn into a dog person and laughingly admitted he didn't think I'd handle it so well when later that evening Chanook brought his rope to me and dropped it my lap, and I actually played with him like I had been doing it my whole life. Slobber and all.

My heart swelled.

The first time I ever walked a dog in my life was with Chanook. I had babysat Macy, my best friend's dog, but never took her on a walk as we had a large fenced in yard I would let her loose in. But I digress, my son was at work and I was getting antsy, it was a little cloudy but I needed to stretch my legs and figured what better way to test myself and see if I could handle the needs of a dog than by taking him for a walk.

"Chanook, sit." I gave him the signal my son had taught me. He sat. I was amazed. After I attached his leash and grabbed the house keys, I asked him, "Walk? You want to go for a walk?" He ran for the door.

"Chanook. Stay," and he did. He waited calmly for me to lock the front door, and after a deep breath I said, "Okay, let's go" and we did. We did a short walk around one block because I was nervous. Turned out it was in vain. Chanook did not wrap himself around me with his leash. He did not pull me. He did not run away and make me chase him. He simply sniffed what was in his path, looked back at me several times to make sure I didn't get lost, or to make sure I was still there. Perhaps he wanted me to go faster, I'll never know what was going on in his doggy mind. What I do know, is that my first ever dog walking experience was a success. That kernel in the back of my mind moved to my newly melting heart.

After that, his blue eyes melted what was left of any resistance I had about wanting a dog and his endless patience with me made me look forward to our daily walks. I learned on my own how to walk a dog for the first time in my life. I have to give credit where credit is due, my son trained this dog well.

Photo Provided by Evelyn M. Zimmer

After two glorious weeks of relaxation, visiting the local attractions and spending quality time with my son, granddaughter, and Chanook, I had come to a decision. I knew I couldn't live my life without the unconditional love of a dog in my home for the rest of my life. Even the constant vacuuming wasn't that bad.

****

Enter Cash

When I came home and got back to work, I had relayed my experiences to my boss.

"You need a dog," she said in her wisdom. "Lucky for you, your boss will let you bring one to work!" She told me about a no-kill shelter in Southfield that might have a rescue dog for me. So I logged onto their website and started watching and waiting for my dog to appear. Patiently waiting. Honest. Well, my version of patient.

One day almost a month later, a Shih-Tzu mix appeared on the site. He was a male, about five years old, white and liver with a sweet face. I filled out the paperwork and waited to hear back from the shelter. After I had been approved, my boss went with me to the shelter to meet my new dog Cash. I texted my husband with the news. He said this wasn't the time for our family to get a dog and I should wait. Like until we retired in fifteen years and had time for a dog.

On the way there my boss cautioned me to use my head and not my heart and be darn sure he was the dog for me before I made a commitment. I met Cash and we took him outside to spend some time together in the lovely May afternoon. The shelter told me that Cash had issues from his previous owner and didn't like to be held. He didn't like sitting on laps either.

"Kinda defeats the purpose of getting a lap dog doesn't it?" I say to my boss.

"Yep," she didn't need to say more.

While we were outside, a teenage boy and his mother were also looking at another Shih-Tzu that was there. They went home with two dogs that day. It just wasn't meant to be. Cash was not my dog either.

****

Enter Leo

A couple of weeks later, June 8th to be exact, I stumbled across an internet ad for a breeder of purebred Shih-Tzu's in White Lake. I had finally given up on getting a Cava-poo. The images of Shih-Tzu's were what kept catching my eye when I was doing searches. This picture was of a solid liver male, eight weeks old. I sent the breeder an email inquiring if the puppy was still available and that I'd like to come by after work any night that week and see him.

The next day I received an email where she began vetting me. She was a serious breeder and was very concerned that the people she let look at her dogs were not undercover puppy mill people that would take her purebreds and sell them to pet stores. I didn't even know that was a thing.

I got directions and we set up a time for the next evening. I called my husband and told him I'd be late coming home from work because I was gonna go check out a puppy.

"Why are you so insistent on doing this now? We have the commissioning party this Saturday and family coming in from out of town to stay with us. We don't need a dog, we can't afford a dog, we don't have time for a dog." I'm sure he said more, but I'm a bad wife and had my mind on the puppy. That little kernel in my heart had grown into a full on obsession.

"Don't worry, he'll probably be sold by the time I get there. She said she had other people coming by tonight also. I really just want to check out this breeder. She only does one litter a year from her dames. Maybe I can put in a request for a puppy for next year if she checks out legit."

"Uh huh." I insist I heard his eyes roll through the phone.

I swear to all that is holy when I pulled up to the address of the breeder, it was a farm. With horses. And Shih-Tzu's. Nine of them. As it turns out, seven males and two females. Not to mention the puppies.

A woman and her mother were there talking to the lady that I assumed was the breeder. She was telling them no, none of the nine were for sale, in fact, they were all pedigreed show dogs.

I introduced myself and told her I was there to see the solid liver male. All of us went inside to her basement. The farmhouse was a tri-level. Apparently there were two litters available. One litter was ten weeks old, the other eight. She assured us she would not be breeding any more litters that year.

I was in puppy overload, yappy ones, bouncy ones, shy ones...solid white, solid black, liver and white, black and white and a lone solid liver. We all spoke of what we were looking for, how she breeds, what the pedigrees were, any ailments, what food they were given and so on. She showed us around and went back upstairs while all three of us played with the puppies.

I took pictures. I texted them to my husband. He texted back "Cute." This was followed immediately by another text which just said, "No."

I spent another half-hour alternating between watching the solid liver male and discussing the merits of the other puppies with the other women there.

Apparently, they've gotten puppies from this breeder before. The mother's dog had recently passed on and she was looking for a replacement. The daughter wanted a second one to keep her two-year-old Shih-Tzu company.

I picked up the solid liver male and held him away from my body so he was on his back, in my hands. He didn't squirm like some of the others. He just yawned. I turned him over and placed him against my shoulder like a baby. He licked my cheek once and put his head on my shoulder and went to sleep. Walking around with him held like that, I texted my husband with my other hand. The exchange went as follows,

"Today or Thursday?"

"Today or Thursday what?"

"Just answer the question."

"What's the question?"

"Today or Thursday?"

"I don't understand."

I started to get emotional. I set the puppy down in his pen with his sisters. He waddled over to the food dish and ate a little, then drank some water and promptly piddled on the newspaper. The breeder came back downstairs to check on us and see if anyone had made a decision. The daughter of the other woman picked up my puppy and proceeded to compare him to the other puppies.

"He has a hernia..." the blond lady said to the breeder.

"Most of them do. If it doesn't heal on its own by the time they are neutered or spayed, the vet will repair it at that time. It's very common with this breed." The breeder and the mother started talking about when she could take her puppy home.

I left the room and called my husband. *No way* was that *broad* getting *my* puppy. Hubby answered the phone and I jump right in, "I understand everything that you've said and you are absolutely right. The timing is wrong, we can't afford him and I have no idea what I'm doing. But that dog is *mine*, we've bonded and I don't think my heart will take it if I don't bring him home now."

"We've got the commissioning on Saturday. People are staying at our house come Thursday. You have to work tomorrow late and I have to work. There will be no one home to take care of him. You can't do that to a new puppy. It's cruel."

"I can take him to work. My boss said I can."

"We can't afford him."

"Don't care. This is my dog."

"Fine. Do whatever." I really do love that man more than I'll ever let him know.

Walking back into the room I noticed the blond was still holding him but he was squirming a little as if he wanted down. I said to the blond a little more overprotectively than anticipated, "Sorry love, he's mine. May I have him back now?" Then I turned to the breeder and asked her politely what the next steps were. As the lady handed him back to me, he licked my hand and promptly fell asleep on my shoulder again. Yep. He was mine alright. We went upstairs to fill out the paperwork and she gave me an Amazon box with a blanket to put him in. She gave me a container with some homemade puppy food and a bag with a couple of toys. We filled out the paperwork and after some directions on how to prepare the food and when his next shots were due we were on our way.

I put him in the backseat and put the seatbelt around the box, he was as safe as I could make him. Backing out of the driveway of the farm I couldn't believe what I had done. I bought a puppy. Dear God, what do I do now?

What I did next was stop at the first pet supply store I passed. I took my Amazon box into the store with me, placed it in the cart and started panic shopping. I was gonna need a crate, food dishes, a car carrier, a collar, a leash, sweet heavens what have I done?

On the way home with the new love of my life, I talked calmly to him so he would know my voice. I didn't want him to be anxious. You know what? He didn't make a peep all the way home and he didn't have any 'accidents' either.

When I pulled into the garage, my darling hubby helped me bring everything inside and then I took him out of the box and placed him on the kitchen tile. He was so tiny!

Photo Provided by Evelyn M. Zimmer

I shooed away my husband and went into overprotective mode immediately. "Let him get used to the place on his own," I said.

"That isn't a dog Mom, it's a furry rat." My youngest said when he came into the room. He was sooo not pleased with the situation at all. Unless it was a Sheppard or Husky, it just wasn't a dog according to him. My son had wanted a dog his entire life and I was the evil one that always said no. Actually I believe my standard line was, "When you grow up and get a house of your own, you can have as many dogs as you like."

"Don't expect me to take care of it." He fumed further.

"It's my dog, why would I expect you to do anything?" I nipped back. I was very determined to be this puppy's protector and champion.

My new puppy was wagging its tiny tail and sniffing around, then put his little puppy paws on my calf to be picked up. Which of course I did. He licked my hand a few times and then looked over at my husband. I handed him over with trepidation. I was slightly fearful that the new love of my life would prefer my hubby over me.

As I was being lectured on the needs of a new puppy by both my husband and my son, all I heard was the joy in my heart. It had finally happened. I was a dog person.

Now we needed a name for him. My oldest, who was on the phone with my outraged youngest, suggested 'For Sale' as a joke. Both my sons thought that was hysterical. It made me cry. My oldest apologized. My youngest rolled his eyes and said I was being too sensitive.

After two days of trial and error, my husband and I finally decided to name him Leo for his unyielding sense of bravery.

This darling little fellow is a trooper. The next day he came to work with me, neither my boss nor I got much done that day.

The day after that, my out of town family descended and the socializing of Leo began. That Saturday we had a huge commissioning party at our house for our youngest who was becoming an officer in the Marine Corps. Little Leo spent the days running around greeting everyone and when I was afraid he was getting overwhelmed, I placed him in his crate in the kitchen, safe from so many feet and the grabby little hands of my adorable granddaughter, yet still around all the commotion of the party. Did I mention my granddaughter was four at the time?

We were spared the horror story events of the puppy not sleeping at night. Leo spent his very first night in his crate, right next to our bed, without a whimper one. We continued this arrangement of his crate in the kitchen during the day, and in our room at night until our company had gone back home. It was the first night after the company was gone that we had a bit of a hiccup with his sleeping routine. That was the night I decided in all my new found wisdom that his crate should stay in the kitchen permanently.

This arrangement took two nights of calmly telling Leo that this was his special spot and he was safe right where he was. He listened to my tone and accepted what I said at face value. Then he decided to test it. He barked a couple of teeny tiny barks after I had gone back into the bedroom. I'm sure he just wanted to know if I could hear him. I came back out and told him, "Leo, you're fine. Go to sleep honey."

A couple of hours later he did it again. I repeated the speech I gave him earlier and added a pat on the head through the crate. The second night, he barked because I was foolish enough not to potty him first. After taking him out to do his business, he settle down for a long nap. We didn't have any night time barking issues after that.

The following week and through the rest of the summer there was a round of social events at several of my friends' homes. Leo went with me everywhere. I dragged him about just as I did my boys when they were growing up. How else are you going to learn to be a well-adjusted social butterfly? My friends had small dogs too, and they all got along great. Much to my relief.

God truly blessed me with my slow path to Leo. Over the last few months, I have learned to receive and give unconditional love from and to a dog. To not sweat the occasional licking, dog baths, or poop patrol. Most of all that a house littered with dog toys is truly a home worth having.

Leo has been the perfect puppy for me. We learn together. He spends most of his days either playing near me in my office or lounging on my desk, sometimes even on me! This little darling is very interested in whatever I may be doing. I'm grateful he is not yappy nor is he high strung and he tolerates everyone he comes across. By the way, he has charmed our mail lady too. She leaves treats in our mailbox for him every day! Even the UPS man thinks he rocks.

Leo is a consummate traveler. He took two trips up north with me on 'girlfriend weekends' to my friend's cabin, which is four hours away, that summer. He was a perfect gentleman and made me so proud that he has been invited back anytime.

Then this past fall my husband and I took Leo on his first really long trip. We took a car trip to San Antonio, which was two extremely long days in the car both ways. I'm happy to report he had zero 'accidents' in the car, and he never seems to get annoyed with us about travel. But that's a story for another time.

I wish I could say I was diligent with his training, but after sit, and stay, and teaching him to stop at the corners when we go for walks, his training took a fanciful bent. I taught him to dance. His little dance moves on his hind legs causes me such overwhelming joy that I have to pick him up and hug him. Every single time. In fact, Leo humors me several times a day with this trick.

If there is a downside to being Leo's human, it's that he has zero loyalty. He loves everyone. Especially my husband. For a man that kept saying 'no' he's terribly happy we have him now!

As I write the end of this piece Dear Reader, Leo is nestled on my lap and contentedly earning his keep as my lap dog. This was definitely one of my better decisions, I must admit. It really is Puppy Love!

The Siberian Queen
By Gaye Buzzo Dunn

Kasha, my new Siberian Husky pup, peed in the car's back seat all the way to her new home in Southwest Florida. A previous Husky owner, I knew that young Huskies are frightened when first separated from their pack. Taken from her Dam and fellow littermates, I understood this trauma on her first day of separation. However, perhaps this was a warning that Kasha's life might be more interesting than the average dog.

Born in Ocala, Florida to purebred registered parents; Kasha was sable and white in color, rare for her breed. Right from the start she exhibited independence and confidence—a beautiful female puppy that would eventually grow into a handsome dog. Once acclimated to her surroundings, she was a joyful pet. Our two daughters romped with her when she tagged along to the school bus stop. The other children petted and lavished her with attention until the bus arrived and Kasha and I returned home. Despite all this loving attention, before long small incidents began to occur.

Kasha was oblivious to our golfing community deed restrictions. She could care less that all homes had to remain unfenced and pets must be contained and adhere to community leash laws. The first time she slipped out the back door she scampered around the golfers on the 17th tee box until a player saw me running and brought her back. No harm done—yet. I installed a run line in our small back yard, tried to walk her as much as possible, but crafty Kasha continued to find escape opportunities. How could I keep her confined to a small yard once she'd discovered eighteen holes on a golf course? Despite the family's herculean efforts to keep her contained, she always managed to find a way out. Thank goodness my husband's work transfer facilitated a family move before passionate golfers complained and we incurred a hefty fine.

The new home, an older house with a long fenced-in two acre back yard was perfect for Kasha and our two young daughters. After we had settled in, I thought Kasha might benefit from some companionship. I adopted Brandy, a Black Labrador, who joined Kasha in the yard. When Kasha grew larger, she grew intolerant of Brandy's company. The two dogs constantly fought with Kasha showing disdain for Brandy's poop-eating habit. The disharmony was tumultuous, to say the least. Exhausted from the frequent turmoil, I found a new home for Brandy on a nearby farm and months later heard she was thriving and happily rolling around in the owner's pasture. Peace reigned again at our house.

I should have left Kasha alone but I didn't. A dog lover with a soft spot for orphans, I brought home two Malamute/Husky mixed males. Wild pups, Boris and

Dogma, gravitated toward Kasha, a substitute mother figure. Boris, the larger, stronger male, and Kasha hit it off; very soon he became the favorite. Kasha tolerated Dogma, but any stupid move on Dogma's part was met with a swift snap to his snout. Boris was twice Kasha's size with jaws that could crush her in one bite, but he peed in fright if Kasha so much as looked at him with a threatening glance. There was no doubt that Kasha was the reigning, dominant dog of the group. All remained calm once they accepted the living arrangements until I made the greatest mistake. I thought adding another female would be a good balance: two males, two females. I was so wrong.

I just couldn't resist little Genevieve, a Siberian, who had yet to achieve her full growth. Kasha hated Genevieve from the first moments of her arrival. Kasha bit, snarled at and stole Genevieve's treats whenever my back was turned. Again there was continual friction between the two females while Boris and Dogma stood by not willing to join the fray. When Genevieve, no match for Kasha, reached her full growth and gradually accepted her place, the yard again settled into a more placid routine. However, there was no doubt that Kasha was Queen of the realm and Boris her King. Overall, they were good dogs well-loved by our family and I relaxed knowing four pets were enough. And then the first unexpected incident occurred.

There was a breakout. Kasha and Boris went missing. Genevieve, who never followed Kasha and Dogma with his weak hind leg, remained in the yard. My phone rang. The call came from a frightened, Mexican neighbor a mile down the road. In broken English and a panicked voice, he told me my "wolves" were hanging out in his back yard (he read my telephone number from Boris's collar). I arrived at his house, stuffed my bad dogs in the car, apologized profusely while handing him a twenty dollar bill hoping to soothe his jangled nerves— no language barrier there—and returned home. I was very angry. The more I thought about this episode I knew it couldn't have been Kasha that instigated the escape. Kasha was content roaming within her large domain; it had to be Boris. Still upset, I confined both dogs to the smaller enclosure until the weekend when we installed electricity on the fence. This was not going to happen again.

But it did. Unfortunately one evening when my daughter, Anna, put the trash out for collection the lid was loose and the aroma of turkey dinner scraps must have been too good to resist. This time it was Kasha who leaped over the fence. Garbage bags, wrappers, turkey bones, cans and food particles were strewn in a trail down the driveway and Kasha had disappeared. It wasn't long before the phone rang this time from County Animal Control. They brought Kasha home in the doggy paddy wagon and presented me with a hefty fine. And that wasn't the end of it. After animal control left a lady in a gray pick-up truck pulled into the scrap strewn driveway, her left hand dangled outside the driver side window holding a bloody, dead chicken. She advised me her chicken was a layer and was already quoting the cost of her lost egg income. She threatened to sue. I paid the fine; wrote the lady a hundred dollar check for lost egg money and after she left, ignoring the messy driveway, sat outside on a stool and cried. I had to do something.

It turned out I didn't have to supercharge a taller fence. Another business transfer expected to last three to five years came through and the family had to move to the northeast climate of New York State. Sadly, this meant I had to consider downsizing our pets. When the time came for the move, although it broke my heart, new homes with two loving families were found for Genevieve and Dogma. Only Kasha and Boris would be coming with us. I hoped they would adjust to the new environment and climate.

Kasha and Boris were somewhat disoriented, but we kept a close watch on them while we installed an underground fence. They did break out once before the fence installation was complete and fully charged but were quickly recovered. A new neighbor did tell me that the dogs ran through her yard and her children were fearful of our wolf dogs. She hoped they weren't "vicious." I assured her they weren't and invited her and the children over to meet the dogs and our two girls. She declined.

There were a few incidents during the New York stay. Additional training, a highly charged fence and the aging of the dogs made the stay mostly trouble-free. However, Kasha was bored and unhappy confined to smaller quarters. One day I caught her with a skeletal cat arm in her mouth and found cat bones under the back deck. Kasha looked both guilty and pleased. My guess is that a stray cat somehow came into her territory and met its fate. When our work project in New York ended and relocation was pending back to Southern Florida, I had to make a decision about the welfare of our pets. It was painful, but we had to give up the dogs.

Kasha was not happy in enclosed small areas and I could no longer consider a large acreage for her and Boris. It was painful, but I gave up both dogs for adoption. I cried when they left, but stopped by and checked on them in their new homes twice before the relocation. Boris was doing well, and Kasha seemed taken with the young son in the family that adopted her. They bonded well, or so I thought.

Many months later my phone rang in Florida. An animal control officer from New York had located me through the chip in Kasha's ear. Kasha was discovered in a ditch unable to walk. A family reported they found her at the end of their driveway in the pouring rain trying to drink rain water out of a puddle. My heart ached. How did this happen? I advised the officer that Kasha had been adopted by a local New York family and I was now living in Florida. He asked me what he should do.

I couldn't leave Kasha weak and sick on the side of a road. I asked the officer to bring her to the local veterinarian that had previously cared for her. I tried to reach the adopted family only to find the telephone had been disconnected. I assumed the family might have abandoned her and she was trying to return home to us. Kasha's injuries were minor taking only a couple of weeks to heal; she regained her strength and was soon ready to leave the animal hospital. I spoke with the veterinarian, sent him a check for airfare and together we arranged for Kasha's direct flight from New York to Florida.

I'm sure the flight in the cargo hold was frightening but as soon as Kasha saw me waiting at the airport we had a grand reunion. Kasha, older and more mature now, was a changed dog. I sensed her fear in being separated from us again and she settled in the small yard without complaint. We did install an underground fence again just to be prudent but this time I wasn't concerned about Kasha trying to escape. I introduced her to the new neighbors, brought her to the bus stop to get acquainted with the neighbor kids just as I did when she was a pup. However, I did have one small concern.

Priscilla. The girls missed the dogs and after another move, hopefully this time for good, they asked— actually begged for a kitten. Instead I adopted Priscilla, a young, mixed breed, take no prisoners cat. A smarty pants kitty, I believed she was clever enough to keep her distance or perhaps even dethrone our Siberian Queen. Time will tell.

Who Rescued Whom?

By Susan Anmuth

The decision to adopt Tatiana, a senior Yorkshire terrier, remains the most consistent source of joy of my life. We've been together five years.

Photo Provided by Susan Anmuth

I have a grown son I adore. I have close friends and assorted relatives I love. But no relationship with another human being—a person as complicated and as themselves as you are complicated and yourself—can be forever blissful.

That's what dogs are for.

As a child who loved animals, I desperately wanted a pet. The wish, the need, was denied. Because-we-say-so denied. But I knew my parents would get me a puppy for my tenth birthday because they promised I'd be thrilled with their gift.

The present turned out to be a Mickey Mouse watch.

For reasons never clarified, we did finally get a dog. Too, too late. I was sixteen and in full dating throes. Moreover, Duchess was the exact wrong kind of dog a beagle mix who liked everyone equally. Unless you were trying to move her so you could get under the bedcovers. Then she growled. Her one attraction was that walking her at night provided the means to sneak-meet my boyfriend, Chic. My parents disapproved of Chic because he was a few years older, in the army, and most especially, very not Jewish. *Presbyterian*.

You'd think I'd get my own dog when I moved out of the house. But life intervened. I lived in Manhattan apartments, by definition tiny, and went to school and worked and had a dramatic love life and got involved in the anti-Vietnam War and Women's Liberation movements and remain socially active to this day. Had a husband, had a kid, had plenty of personality full cats over the years, but never had time or space for a dog.

For my sixtieth birthday, I decided to finally give myself the gift I'd always wanted.

I worked then in the finance department of a major New York City animal welfare association. I'd been complaining that adoptable dogs in the shelter were big, mostly pit bulls, and I wanted a small dog. A veterinarian mentioned that a Yorkie had been brought in so recently she wasn't on anyone's radar. I called, emailed, and called again to lock down an employee foster hold. That meant that the organization would pay for Tatiana's extensive medical care, I would nurse her when she was released, and then adopt or bring her back ready for adoption.

The trustee who organized the institution's most lucrative annual fundraiser happened to pass through the shelter and spy my Tati. She said, "Wait! This is exactly what I need as my bicoastal dog! Small enough to fly with me between Long Island and Los Angeles!" She proposed to adopt her immediately, covering all medical costs herself.

This put me under heavy pressure to give Tatiana up. But fuggedaboutit. I generously offered to bring my dog to this woman's mansion for play dates. I further explained I would not object if she wanted to pay the vet bills.

That turned out not to be her interest.

Meanwhile, I visited Tatiana in her enclosure. Estimated to be ten years old, she was seriously indifferent to human contact. She weighed only 3.1 pounds and was too despondent to eat. If I hadn't seen the dog food surrounding her, I'd swear they were starving her. The only time her ears pricked up was when another dog barked. I visited again. She was no more responsive. What had I gotten myself into? I asked Trish, the animal behaviorist, if this animal would ever bond with anyone. Trish thought about it before she shrugged.

The day came for Tatiana's release. A double radical mastectomy had eradicated numerous tumors, both malignant and benign. She was on antibiotics for a urinary infection. Did I mention she had no teeth? And because of this, the bone structure couldn't hold so her tiny jaw was fractured in multiple places.

I was terrified. I typed out a list of questions, including how much and what kind of food to feed her, how to avoid breaking her little legs, and when her next check-up should be scheduled. Lindsey, the adoptions vet technician, was both patient and pointed about my anxiety. Her most useful advice was, "Don't coax her to eat. Just throw the food away after half an hour and put out more at the next mealtime." Unless you've parented a picky eater child, you have no idea how difficult it is to follow this counsel.

It was raining that night, typical early November gloom. Getting Tatiana home, in an orange patterned carrier donated by a friend, involved bus, subway, New Jersey transit, and one more bus. On every mode of transportation, I kept the carrier unzipped and caressed her little head, crooning songs I'd sung twenty years previously to my son. "I love you, a bushel and a peck. I love you with a hug around the neck. I... LOVE ... YOU."

This being New York, no other passenger lifted an eyebrow. Neither did Tatiana.

The last part of the trip from Far Upper East Side, New York to Ironbound Newark, New Jersey meant walking a few wet blocks from the bus stop and up two flights of stairs. "We're hooooommmee, sweetie," I informed Tatiana, expecting her to hide for hours; I was bracing myself to leave her alone. I gently put the carrier down, allowing our cat Jelly to sniff it. I carefully opened one end. Tatiana slid out, took a long, luxurious stretch and a long, luxurious pee right on the spot. Tail up, she marched around inspecting her new home. This was too much for Jelly, who chased the interloper. Tati came straight to me.

From that moment on, she was my dog.

Tatiana is completely my girl yet is sweet and sociable to everyone. Walking her is an exercise in rolling waves of ahhhhhh's. She reaps plenty of attention from kids on the street and old men smoking cigars on park benches and couples ambling hand in hand. Sometimes when a cute guy says, "How adorable!" I respond, "Thanks! And my dog is too, right?" I tell giggling toddlers they may pet her, gently. When they do I say, "She likes you! She likes how gentle you are." Their mothers thank me in Portuguese, the language of choice in my section of Newark.

Tati's not a dog's dog. In princess-like manner, she disdains those that jostle around, sniffing that canine anal gland which is as individual as a human fingerprint.

It's only when a dog displays no interest that Tatiana wants to touch noses.

On the home front, Tatiana and Jelly are frenemies. The cat is justifiably jealous. She used to be an only pet. I can identify, being the oldest sibling in my family, but can't help being madly in love with my dog. I tell Jelly I love her too, but she isn't fooled. She knows there's no comparison. In compensation, she's become the Evil Einstein of cats, every waking moment she spends thinking up new ways to torture Tatiana. While the dog is peacefully drinking water, Jelly sneaks up and nips her on the hind leg. While Tati is curled on one of five thousand pet beds scattered around the apartment, the cat pushes her out to take over that particular bed, overflowing its sides and grinning a wicked pussycat grin. The only thing Tatiana protects from Jelly is her food. Thus, the cat plays a good role in encouraging my now five-pounder to eat.

Unlike the stereotype, my dog and I look nothing alike, but we share certain traits. For instance, Tatiana's sense of direction is as challenged as my own. Since she can't quite see through thickening cataracts, when we're at someone's house she snuffles a lot of people's shoes as she searches for me. Our short-term memories are similar as well. She often forgets where I was when she checked five minutes before.

What I love about Tati's tail is its honesty. It's a straight up little stump as she's happily exploring my friend Irene's big yard or while protecting me with deep barks and quivering body against those scary toll collectors on the New Jersey Turnpike. Yes, yes, I keep forgetting to get EZPass, and Tatiana's one imperfection is her failure to remind me. But when she fears that my flinging clothes into a suitcase might mean abandonment, the tail flags. She never pretends cheer.

On walks, the leash suddenly tugs as if I've landed a fifty pound trout. I look down to see Tati looking up, patiently explaining, "This is where we stop to sniff and pee. You knew that, right?" I love that she thinks I know everything.

Tatiana is very precise about her wishes. While I'm driving, she stretches out on my lap. If I happen to stroke her and she's not in the mood, she stands up, gives me a look, and hops onto the passenger seat. After a moment, she gives me another look to emphasize that sleeping on me is one thing, but kindly keep my hands on the wheel. Then she hops back and drapes back over me. I delight in my dog's sassy independence.

I wish I were as endearing as she is. I'll go further in some ways I'd like to be my dog, and I wish other people were too. The sense in which this is most true, besides of course, her inextinguishable loyalty, is that Tatiana judges not by appearance. In fact, dogs are clueless about frivolities like relative size, color, and breed. Why is it we humans are so focused on whether a calf is nicely rounded, a waist is willowy or a man's shoulders are broad? Really, what does it matter, compared to their kindness or sense of humor?

Okay, I said Tati is an unalloyed joy. But I lied. The not-fun part is her mortality. Damn pets for having shorter life spans than we do!

This is what I did for Tatiana before seven AM today. I gave her amoxicillin for a tummy bacterial infection. I squirted 1.5 mg of Benazepril down her reluctant throat. Benazepril is a high blood pressure medication used to manage chronic renal disease, which my dog developed a few years ago. One mg of famotidine followed the Benazepril. Famotidine is like Pepcid and helps prevent the ulcers that can form because kidney failure causes urea to accumulate in the blood.

Then I crushed one-quarter pill of an appetite enhancer, mirtazapine, sprinkling the white dust into baby chicken food on top of Tati's regular prescribed kidney-sensitive food, which currently she's boycotting. Hence the appetite enhancer. I wash my hands thoroughly because I need the opposite of an appetite enhancer. I put a Cyclosporine Ophthalmic drop into each eye since she doesn't produce enough moisture, especially in her left. And I also mixed into the baby food a crumbled half tablet of joint medicine which I give her every other day.

Tonight she'll get only the antibiotic and an extra dose of Pepcid. I'm supposed to moisten her eyes twice a day but Tati hates it so I rarely do. The vet said she can live with a consistent once a day dose. It's hard to maintain twice a day eye drops because they seem so ineffectual. So I compromise between doing my duty and being inhibited by a feeling of profound uselessness.

Really, though, the daily meds drill is not that big a deal—not compared with the daily joys. Tatiana is always thrilled when I walk through the door, dancing on hind legs in her circus poodle impression, wiggling all over, turning her body so I'll deliver her favorite butt rub. Every morning she hip hops from the pillow we've shared all night, my cheek pressing her flank, and greets the day with a down doggy bow.

Tatiana showers me with the 'you-are-perfectly-perfect' devotion that only a one-person dog can pull off—despite all evidence of my imperfections. She makes me very happy.

Contributing

Authors

Susan Anmuth

Susan lives in Newark, New Jersey with her son Ethan, their cat Jelly, and their Yorkie pup Xena the Warrior Princess. Tatiana died at age fifteen and a half last May. Even Jelly was distraught. Xena is the opposite of Tati: a tornado with teeth.

Edited by Evelyn M. Zimmer

Puppy Love: 2015

Gary Beck

Gary has spent most of his adult life as a theater director, and as an art dealer when he couldn't make a living in the theater. He has eleven published chapbooks and one other accepted for publication. His original plays and translations of *Moliere, Aristophanes and Sophocles* have been produced Off-Broadway. Gary's poetry, fiction, and essays have appeared in hundreds of literary magazines. Mr. Beck currently lives in New York City.

Edited by Evelyn M. Zimmer   Puppy Love: 2015

Linda Carol Cobb

Linda, a retired high school teacher, sponsored an award-winning newsmagazine, coached forensics and taught journalism, advanced composition, and public speaking, among other English electives. In retirement, she teaches seminars at The Muse Writing Center, copyedits and coaches public speaking. Her work has appeared in Writers Haven Magazine and *America's Got Stories*. Linda is writing a collection of short, true stories about her experiences and her quirky Tennessee family.

Edited by Evelyn M. Zimmer

Puppy Love: 2015

Thomas Ford Conlan

Tom lives, writes, and tends grape vines in the highlands of Northern Michigan. He has captained a Coast Guard Cutter, sailed the world's lakes and oceans, and fished the rivers and streams of North America. Tom's work appears in Vine Leaves Literary Journal, Issue #12, and he currently serves as nonfiction genre editor for Qu, A Literary Journal. Tom holds a Master of Fine Arts in Creative Writing from Queens University of Charlotte, and a Master of Science from the US Naval Postgraduate School in Monterrey, California.

Frances G. Dunn

Gaye Buzzo Dunn is a passionate short story writer, a so-so golfer, and an avid gardener. She's happiest with a pen, golf club or garden trowel held in her left hand. You can find further information on Gaye's published work at: www.penandpatience.wordpress.com. The Siberian Queen is dedicated to my daughter, Shelley Dunn.

Sharon Frame Gay

Sharon grew up a child of the highway, traveling throughout the United States, playing by the side of the road. Her dream was to live in a house long enough to find her way around in the dark, and she has finally achieved this outside Seattle, Washington. Sharon writes poetry, prose, short stories and song lyrics.

Robert Iulo

Robert is retired from a career with the City of New York. His work has appeared in *The Museum of Americana, Epiphany Magazine, Gastronomica* among others, and he's had a special feature about his volunteer work after Katrina published in *The Mississippi Sun Herald*. Robert is a native New Yorker and still lives in New York City.

Edited by Evelyn M. Zimmer

Laurie Kolp

Laurie serves as president of Texas Gulf Coast Writers and gathers monthly with other local members of the Poetry Society of Texas. Her poems have appeared in more than four dozen print and online journals, anthologies and magazines worldwide, including the *2015 Poet's Market* and Diane Lockward's *The Crafty Poet*. You can find further information on Laurie's published works at: http://www.lauriekolp.com.

Gerri Leen

Gerri lives in Northern Virginia and originally hails from Seattle. She is editing an anthology, *A Quiet Shelter There*, which will benefit homeless animals and is due out in 2015. You can find further information on Gerri's published works at: http://www.gerrileen.com.

Stephanie Madan

Stephanie is a columnist for the print magazine *My Table*, a column for which she received a 2014 Lone Star Award. She also has poetry published in Texas Poetry Calendar 2015. Stephanie shares her days with her husband and two white dogs – a qualified white as they are tomboys and remind many of walking trash cans with animated tails.

E. Suzin Odlen

Suzin received a BS from Temple University and an MA from Rowan University. She is a retired casino cocktail waitress who lives near Atlantic City, New Jersey with her Golden Retriever, Derby. Her most recent publications appear in the *New York Times, Boston Literary Magazine, Postcard Shorts, Red Fez, and Vine Leaves Literary Journal.* Suzin is a Pushcart Prize nominee.

Andrea Onstad

Several of Andrea's monologs have appeared in collections published by *Heinemann and Applause Books*. Her plays have been produced in various venues in the United States and Germany. Andrea currently live in an off-the-grid cabin in Northern California.

Edited by Evelyn M. Zimmer

Lisa Reinhardt

Lisa grew up in Chappaqua, New York and moved to California in 1993. She landed just over the Golden Gate Bridge in Marin County where she went to school nights and at the age of forty-two earned a Bachelor's Degree in writing from Dominican University. After a long career in advertising as a design studio manager, she is writing again. This is her first published piece. Lisa and her dog Molly live in Portland, Oregon now where she is also a volunteer for the Oregon Humane Society.

Allan Rozinski

Allan lives in Selinsgrove, Pennsylvania with Webster his Boston terrier. He has a Bachelor of Science degree in secondary education English from Bloomsburg University in Pennsylvania. Allan is primarily a writer of speculative fiction.

Priya Vennapusa

    Priya is a short story and fiction writer who focuses on women and women's perspectives in her writing. She has written most of her life in one form or another and reading is her favorite pastime. She loves romance and comedy both in real life and fiction. One of her favorite quotes is "What is life without love and laughter?" Priya lives in Michigan with her family and her dog.

Matthew Wilson

Matthew has had over 150 appearances in such places as *Horror Zine, Star*Line, Spellbound, Illumen, Apokrupha Press, Hazardous Press, Gaslight Press, Sorcerers Signal* and many more. He is currently editing his first novel.

Evelyn M. Zimmer

Evelyn began her writing career in the second half of her life. While she has always had a love affair with the written word, it wasn't until now that she has had the time to dedicate herself to her passion. In her spare time, she enjoys various activities with her friends and visiting her family across the States. Evelyn lives in her family home in Michigan with her husband Paul and the newest addition to their family, a Shih-Tzu named Leo.